**"I have to run," Pilar said. "You too.
Get in your truck and leave town."**

"What about you?"

"I'll have to go on foot. My car's in the back."

They both froze at the sound of the kitchen doorknob being jiggled. Pilar pressed her hand across her mouth, her skin a ghastly pallor.

Austin knew what he had to do, as much as it pained him. "Come on. I'll drive you," he whispered.

"No..." she said, so low he almost missed it.

"Seems to me you don't have another option," he tossed over his shoulder. "It's not what I want either, but you're not going to get far on foot in this storm."

Still she stood rooted, backpack dangling from her fingers, until there was a crash of a fist coming through a glass pane. They both ran to the front door; Austin flung it open and hurtled down the stairs into the pouring rain. At the street, he yanked open the door of his truck. Leaping behind the wheel, his heart sank.

Pilar was gone. Again.

Dana Mentink is a nationally bestselling author. She has been honored to win two Carol Awards, a HOLT Medallion and an RT Reviewers' Choice Best Book Award. She's authored more than thirty novels to date for Love Inspired Suspense and Harlequin Heartwarming. Dana loves feedback from her readers. Contact her at danamentink.com.

Visit the Author Profile page at LoveInspired.com for more titles.

DEATH VALLEY DOUBLE CROSS

DANA MENTINK

LOVE INSPIRED SUSPENSE
INSPIRATIONAL ROMANCE

LOVE INSPIRED® SUSPENSE
INSPIRATIONAL ROMANCE

ISBN-13: 978-1-335-73605-5

Death Valley Double Cross

Copyright © 2022 by Dana Mentink

This edition published by arrangement with Harlequin Books S.A.

For questions and comments about the quality of this book, please contact us at CustomerService@Harlequin.com.

Love Inspired
22 Adelaide St. West, 41st Floor
Toronto, Ontario M5H 4E3, Canada
www.LoveInspired.com

Printed in U.S.A.

But he giveth more grace. Wherefore he saith,
God resisteth the proud, but giveth grace unto the humble.
—*James* 4:6

To the National Park Service, who seeks to preserve the precious gift of Death Valley National Park for everyone to enjoy.

ONE

"You have a face only a mother could love, Chunk." Austin Duke peered through the bars of the animal carrier at the roly-poly dog with the pink tongue hanging out the gap where several front teeth had once been. His graying jowls spoke of a pug heritage mixed with something else. Chunk had already lost his beloved elderly owner, been shuttled from shelter to shelter and barely recovered from a bad case of kennel cough. The poor thing hadn't even protested when Austin secured him for the journey, and he'd been a model passenger.

Now Chunk's saggy brown gaze looked so forlorn from behind the bars that Austin could not take another moment. He figured the little guy had been caged long enough, since they'd been driving for more than four hours with only occasional pit stops. There was nothing worse, Austin was certain, than being stuck. He did not let his mind complete the comparison...*just like you.*

He rolled his ruined shoulder and received a jolt of pain for his effort. It wasn't the time to contemplate his life wreckage at the moment. "Want to ride shotgun, old fella?"

Pulling the truck over, he freed Chunk from his carrier, clipped his harness to the belt and made a bed of his fleece jacket on the passenger seat. Before they loaded up again, they both enjoyed a stretch break as they took in the surroundings...a small nondescript community near the Stillwater ghost town in Nevada, the last leg of their journey from Furnace Falls in Death Valley. It was quiet, eerily so.

"You feel better now, sweetie pie?" Austin crooned. He would never use such outrageous baby talk in public, but he turned into a marshmallow around dogs, especially senior ones. That probably explained why he was a volunteer delivery guy for a service that matched sad old pups with people willing to adopt them. Most of the dogs had mobility problems...another comparison he would not indulge in. He could have flown his small plane as he usually did, but due to Chunk's lung condition, the vet discouraged it. Road trip, it had to be. Why not? Spring in Death Valley was always full of surprises.

Chunk's sigh ruffled his lips as he sank into a furry puddle and promptly went to sleep. The snoring commenced immediately. Austin was glad to see the dog resting comfortably. Since his doting owner had passed away, fourteen-year-old Chunk was adrift in the world, pining for his lost companion, shuttled from place to place until he landed at the Furnace Falls shelter.

"Things are looking up, boy, don't you worry." Austin admired the kind soul who had agreed to adopt the dog via Sunshine Senior Dog Rescue.

A kind soul... He couldn't help the image that popped into his mind, blond-haired, soft-spoken Pilar. She would love any creature in the universe wholeheartedly.

Except you, Austin. She stopped loving you, didn't she?

The inevitable depressing wave of memories spooled through his mind. Her crumpled wedding veil on the floor of the church, and the scattered pink petals from the bouquet she'd dropped as she fled. And what had he gotten by way of explanation? A text, of all things. Not even the courtesy of a phone call. I hope you can forgive me someday.

Forgive?

In the past six months since the debacle, his humiliation and hurt had given way to anger, a hard slab of it that lived in his heart under the genial, good-natured demeanor. Outwardly, he fought to be the same upbeat carpenter, quick to laugh, hungry for life and adventure. Inside, he didn't even recognize his own thoughts anymore.

Pilar, his betrayer. If she hadn't wanted to marry him, he could have thought up a good dozen ways she could have broken it to him without running from the altar like a scalded cat. Sure they'd had their problems, plenty of them since he'd wrecked his shoulder the year before, but he'd had no clue she was about to bolt.

No clue? He couldn't quite make himself believe the lie. He'd hurt her plenty, trying to deal with his own mess. Still, there was no excuse for what she'd done.

Another memory, the two of them, discussing wallpaper for the house they would build someday. "Stripes," he'd said. "Floral," she'd come back with at exactly the same moment. And his ears still rang with the sound of their laughter. Little had he known that she would dump him at the altar a few months later, sending the ring back via the mail, post-marked from a town he'd never heard of, no return address.

He cleared his throat and turned on the windshield wipers. March weather in the Mojave Desert was unpredictable, and lately March storms had deluged Death Valley and beyond, including this gloomy Nevada town. He peered through the downpour as they closed in on their destination. Not much to see except an unimpressive main street that opened up into a small suburbia with aged apart-ments and single-family homes. He was surprised at the address on the paperwork he'd been given for Chunk's new owner.

An apartment? No yard for a dog to run around? Of course Chunk wasn't exactly a ball of energy, and small dogs could be happy with apartment living. When they finally arrived, the dog was snoring at an unbelievable volume. He consulted his paperwork. "Well, C. Bolt, whoever you are, I hope you have a good set of earplugs." He parked.

The apartment looked like it had fallen upon hard times, the front window curtains tattered and the rocker on the front porch falling to bits. Concerning. Did the owner understand the medical bills that could sometimes accompany a senior dog adoption? The only bright spot in the scene was a sizzling pink flowering plant that he could not identify, but botanist Pilar would have known in a second. It was sprouting from a repurposed, hand-painted teapot.

You've got to believe in tomorrow if you're a gardener, she'd said.

Tomorrow? She must have believed in a tomorrow that didn't include him. *You're not thinking about her anymore, remember?*

Wind blew wet leaves along the street. He felt a tingle of tension. Why? Nothing amiss on this quiet street. Yet, something seemed off. If he'd decided to fly the dog in his small plane, he would have been checking the plane twice, every light, every switch, until he identified the source of his unease. But his pilot's instinct for trouble seemed like straight up paranoia in this slice of suburbia.

He rechecked the address on the printed email confirmation. *Adoptee: C. Bolt, 300 West Sycamore, Unit 2.* He shoved the paperwork in his back pocket, went around to the passenger side and picked up the sleepy dog. His shoulder twanged with pain, but he kept right on ignoring it. "Not my job to question your new digs, Chunk. I'm just the delivery guy." Chunk waggled his tail in a propeller-like motion. Tucking the dog under his arm football style, he strolled up the warped steps, speckled by the paint peeling off the eaves. Surprisingly, the doorbell was new, one of those fancy camera types. He also noted a sticker for an alarm company on the curtained window.

Security conscious.

"Well, if they're expecting you to perform guard dog activities, we might need to talk them out of that," he said to Chunk.

He thumbed up his baseball cap and rang the bell.

There was no answer, but he was sure he heard someone moving inside. Or maybe he felt it? The first spit of rain hit his cheek. It wouldn't be good for Chunk to get wet, in his fragile condition. Again he felt the flush of unease.

He rang a second time, speaking into the doorbell camera. "Hello? I'm a volunteer with Sunshine Senior Dog rescue. I brought the dog you arranged to adopt."

Nothing.

He tried knocking. No response. "Hmm. Looks like we might have a situation here, Chunk."

Chunk let out a soft whine and started to tremble. Austin cuddled him closer, pulling his windbreaker around the dog. His uncertainty flared higher. If things weren't right, he would simply take the dog home. What was one more pet when he already had three? Not like he was traveling anywhere anytime soon. His sister, Willow, would tease him but fall in love with the dog anyway.

Two more knocks with no response. He pulled out his cell and dialed the number on the email confirmation. One shrill ring sounded inside before the phone was silenced.

So there was somebody inside who'd just shut off their cell phone rather than talk to him? Irritation flashed along his nerves. He had the cell phone number right, so was he being pranked? And who would do that to a poor, elderly dog with nowhere to go? "Mr. or Ms. Bolt? Are you in there?"

The seconds ticked by. He knew someone was inside, he could feel it. He tried to explain the situation again, speaking louder over the rain. Once more there was no answer. Austin shot a glance at a black sedan that drove down the street, windshield wipers clacking now that the rain was falling in earnest. He caught a whiff of cigar smoke through the slightly open window. It reminded him of his cigarette smoking days, a teen trying to be cool in front of his buddies. The car disappeared around the corner.

"All right, fine," he said loudly. "I guess you changed your mind about the dog. You could have called instead of put him through a four-hour drive."

He felt like an idiot talking to a doorbell, holding an elderly dog tight to his chest as he shielded him from the moisture. Chunk let out a quiet whimper. "It's okay, baby," he whispered softly. "I'll take care of you."

He was about to leave when the light on the doorbell blinked and a high tinny voice spoke. "Who are you?"

He'd made contact. Excellent. "Name's Austin. I'm with Sunshine Dog Rescue."

"Who gave you this address?"

"I thought you did." He waved the paper. "Is there someone with the last name of Bolt here?"

There was a long pause before the voice answered.

"No. I'm sorry."

Sorry. Something in the voice, the tone. Had the curtains twitched? The back of his neck prickled, but there was nothing to be done. It wasn't as if he could force whoever it was to open the door. If they didn't want the dog, Chunk was better off without them, but they could have called to cancel, rather than pretending he'd got it all wrong.

The dark sedan appeared once again, trailing a stink of cigar smoke. Now the flutter of unease turned into a flash of foreboding. What was going on here? Whatever it was, he didn't want to stick himself and an elderly dog in the middle of it. Adventure he loved. Drama, not so much.

"Can you at least confirm your cell

phone number? I don't want to keep bothering you if we got it wrong." He began to rattle off the numbers.

He hadn't finished reciting from the delivery form when the front door opened and a hand yanked him inside. Pain flashed through his shoulder. He stumbled and fell onto the yellowing tile entry, Chunk cocooned against him as the door slammed shut.

She quickly locked the door and raced to the living room and looked out. There it was, the sedan idling in the street. The rain prevented her from identifying the person behind the wheel through the falling rain. But she'd seen that sedan before a few days ago, the driver obscured by a cloud of cigar smoke. It wasn't necessary to see his face to make the identification. Her heart thunked, overwhelmed by the car in the street and the man on the floor. What had she done pulling him into the house? But she couldn't let him rattle off her cell phone number without the sedan driver hearing, and he didn't seem to be in any hurry to leave.

Dumb move. Now she had two problems instead of one.

She stayed to the side of the window, not daring to turn around to look. Finally, the sedan drove slowly away leaving her confused. Had she been wrong? Was it an innocent situation? A driver stopped to check a text? Paranoia? She was not sure she would be able to separate legitimate fear from paranoia even if her life depended on it, which it very well might.

She heard him get to his feet before he plunged into the living room, toting the dog.

"Do you always greet people by yanking them into your house?" he demanded.

She squeezed past him into the hallway where the twin mirrors reflected a terrified face from the white painted frames her mother had made. Maybe, just maybe, she looked different enough, her blond hair now black, fifteen pounds thinner thanks to the stress she'd endured, her nose and chin altered by the surgery. She scurried to the kitchen and double-checked that the back door was locked, the kitchen blinds levered closed.

He found her there, leaning against the stove in the dimmest corner. She was sure he must have heard her pulse slamming in her throat as she quickly turned away and fished a backpack out of the cupboard.

"Sorry," she mumbled. "Mistake."

"Do I at least get to know your name?" He put the ball of a dog on the floor.

"Amy."

He cocked his head and looked at her so closely she started to sweat. It would be better, safer for both of them if she could get rid of him before the truth came out. Those same hazel eyes, the strong cheekbones, the hair so blond it was almost white. Nightmare.

"Want to tell me what's going on?" he demanded.

If only she knew. "I didn't ask for a dog." Still angled away from him, she found a bowl, filled it with water and set it next to the pup. He waggled his stump of a tail and slurped it up. She had some dog biscuits in her car, kept there in case she ran across any strays, but she didn't dare go around the back to retrieve any.

The hazel gaze darkened. "You seem familiar. Have we met?"

How she longed to come clean, but she had to do this to protect him, like she'd tried to do all along. She answered with a shake of the head. "Better if you go now," she said, dropping the bottles of water from her last grocery delivery into the pack and adding granola bars and a stray candy bar. Still he stood there, staring.

"Please leave," she said.

Instead, he unfurled a piece of paper with maddening slowness. "Adoptee called in and our secretary took down the info. It's right here. Someone arranged for me to deliver this dog and if it's not you, then how do you explain the address and phone number matching up? I can understand getting one or the other wrong, but not both. Both of them tell me I'm in the right place and there's something weird going on here. You yanking me into the house is a pretty good indication too."

An engine rumbled outside. Sucking in a breath, she hurried back to the living room and peered out from behind the curtain. The sedan again, driving slowly this time, turning down the alley between her building and the empty lot. Checking out the back where it would be easier to break in? Not her paranoia now. She had to run out the front. Head to the bus station. No choice.

As she sprinted back to the kitchen, she nearly plowed into Austin, who had been eyeing her. He put a hand out to steady her but she pulled back.

"What's wrong?" he demanded.

Skirting around him she called out, "I have to go."

"Why? Who's in the sedan?"

"Not your business. I'm leaving." He'd go now, surely. He'd have to.

She was reaching for the wallet on the table when he got there ahead of her and snatched it up.

Fear nearly choked her. She held out her hand without a word.

After the longest moment of her life, he laid the wallet in her palm. "Are you afraid I might take a look at your ID... Amy?" He leaned forward and looked deeply into her eyes. "Or maybe I should call you Pilar, for old times' sake?"

TWO

He was living a dream, or a nightmare. Pilar Jefferson's pale gray eyes, the eyes that he would never forget, stared at him from a face he did not recognize. The voice though...there was no disguising the soft cadence that was hers and hers alone. A million questions raced through his mind, but he could only manage a single word.

"Why?"

It pinned her in place for only a moment. "I have to run. You too." She bit her lip, body electric with tension. "Get in your truck and leave town."

"What about you?"

"I'll go on foot. My car's in back."

They both froze at the sound of the

kitchen doorknob being jiggled. Pilar pressed her hand across her mouth, her skin a ghastly pallor in the gloom.

Austin thought about his choices, which were not choices at all. He knew what he had to do, as much as it pained him. "Come on. I'll drive you," he whispered as he picked up Chunk and hurried to the front foyer.

"No..." she said, so low he almost missed it.

"Seems to me you don't have another option," he tossed over his shoulder. "It's not what I want either, but you're not going to get far on foot in this storm. You never were one for braving the elements." Uncalled for, to poke her about that, but he couldn't help himself.

Still she stood rooted, backpack dangling from her fingers, until there was a crash of a fist coming through a glass pane. They both ran to the front door, flung open the lock, hurtled down the stairs into the pouring rain. At the street, he yanked open the door of his truck with his good arm and stowed Chunk in his carrier in the cramped space behind the passenger seat. Leaping behind the wheel his heart sank.

Pilar was gone. Again. He saw only a flash of her white sneakers as she scooted up the main street and darted between two buildings. Gunning the engine to life, he gave himself practical advice.

She was in trouble that he knew nothing about. Had she gone so far as to have her face surgically altered?

She'd asked him flat out to leave.

She'd refused to get in the truck.

The smartest thing to do would be to drive away and leave her, as she'd done to him.

Leave her...

They were night and day, he reminded himself. She didn't want the same things he did. The busted marriage ceremony probably saved them both a lot of grief.

Leave...her...

The hard knot in his stomach twisted uncomfortably as he came to a decision.

Muttering, he cranked the wheel and made for the end of the block, windshield wipers slapping ineffectually at the downpour. She'd gone around two commercial buildings that opened into a weedy lot backed by a sort of industrial area. Long stretches of empty pavement interrupted by storage units and scraggly weeds met his searching gaze.

How long would it take for the guy who'd broken the window to ascertain the situation and launch into pursuit mode?

He scanned the blighted landscape. Where had Pilar gone?

More questions followed. What had happened to her? Who was after her? And why?

He hadn't seen her clearly enough to figure out exactly how her face was different, but the fear in her voice was plain as anything. *Not your problem*, his brain repeated ever more stridently, yet his stubborn heart kept the truck inching through the pouring rain. A flash of color snagged his attention, no more than a glimpse. Hitting the brakes, he backed up until he was able to discern her clearly, huddled there between giant storage containers. She was leaning against the wet metal siding, clasping her arm.

He was out of the truck and at her side in two seconds.

She jerked a look at him, brow puckered in pain. "What...what are you doing here?"

He ignored the question and pointed to her arm where the blood showed through a gouge in her jacket sleeve. "Cut?"

For a moment he didn't think she was going to answer. "Caught my arm on a hinge."

"I have a first-aid kit in the truck."

"I..."

"Pilar," he snapped, "I'm tired of standing in the rain. I can't leave you like this."

She no doubt caught the bitterness in his tone. *Leave...like you did to me.*

"Yes, you can," she said, only a shade louder than the rain.

Her expression was stark, desperate and she looked so very broken. His breath caught but he forced a coolness into his voice, a calm he did not feel. "We'll get you patched up and dropped wherever you want to be delivered."

She did not reply, merely looked down at her arm. He waited a moment, but still she did not make a move to follow him.

In a risky maneuver, he turned his back, marched to the truck and yanked open the passenger door. As he turned, he wondered. Would she be there behind him? Or had she taken off yet again?

Neither. When he looked, she was standing still, holding her arm, exactly where he'd found her. The rain sheeted off her jacket and soaked the mane of hair, which six months ago had almost matched his blond. Now it was a raven dark mass of dampening curls that almost reached her shoulders.

Who are you, Pilar?

But he did not ask aloud. Instead, he held his breath and waited to see what choice she would make.

The seconds ticked into a full minute. The answer was clear even if he didn't want to admit it to himself. She hadn't moved and she wasn't going to. Pain carved an aching path through his insides as he closed the door and trudged back to the driver's seat.

What happened to you, Pilar?

He knew he would probably never get the answer to his question as he shifted the truck into Drive.

Pilar stood rooted in the pouring rain. Austin would be better off without her, certainly safer. The cut on her arm ached but nothing like the deep anguish in her chest.

She'd asked God to forgive what she'd

done to Austin, but she could see in his eyes that her hurt had changed him in ways she would never understand. She'd let the love she'd felt for him fade into oblivion, but the shame remained. She'd never even said she was sorry. That last bit hurt worse than any laceration.

Was she being given one last chance to apologize? If he left now, she knew she would never see him again. His truck rolled on, and she saw his eyes seeking her in the rearview mirror...like a request, one final invitation.

And then her sneakers were squeaking on the wet ground as she ran to the truck. Stumbling, skidding, panting, she drew closer until he stopped with a jerk, leaning over and opening the passenger door.

She climbed in, insides quivering.

Mouth tight, he reached behind the seat with a wince of pain and pulled out a first-aid kit. "Let's get you patched up."

"Not here," she said. "Keep driving, okay? Please?"

"Where to?"

"Back to the freeway. You can leave me at the first rest stop." By then she might be able to work up the courage to give him the apology he deserved.

He didn't answer for a moment. "All right. I'll make a bargain with you. I'll do as you say if you answer my questions."

"Three guesses?" As soon as she'd said it, she wished the words stuffed back into her mouth. It was a game they had played. Three questions, three guesses. They'd enjoyed it on many of their hikes when she'd come to Death Valley as part of her college botany studies. He would be scoping out the trail ahead, calculating the most challenging terrain, picking out the best, most wild expanses, while she would have her gaze riveted to the ground, hunting for plant specimens to admire on safe ground. Opposites attracted.

She saw the muscles in his throat move as he swallowed, but he did not look at her. She busied herself stripping off her sodden jacket and pulling up her sleeve to expose the cut.

"Long," he said.

"Not deep, though." With a wipe she cleaned the wound as best she could, wincing at the discomfort.

"First question...why are you pretending to be someone else, Amy?" Sarcasm mixed with curiosity.

What a question to start with. The answer might take a lifetime to fully explain. She tried to put it into one sentence. "My father stole money, and there are people after me who want it back."

"Your father? I thought he died when you were a kid."

"So did I. My mother finally told me the truth because his partner threatened us...the morning of our wedding," she added softly.

His eyebrows lifted nearly to his hairline as he assimilated the information. "Is that why you ran away?"

"It was part of it, but we both know things wouldn't have worked out."

"Don't speak for me, Pilar."

"You told me as much."

"And we got past it, didn't we? We went on to schedule a wedding and everything, or don't you recall?"

Tears stung her eyes. "Please, Austin. Can we skip that part for now?"

His eyes were flint hard. "Did you have plastic surgery to hide from these cohorts of your father's?"

"No." Her breathing went shallow, but she forced herself to answer. "Like I said, my mother had to tell me the truth about my father. He'd been released from prison where he'd served fifteen years for robbing an armored car and injuring the guard. The whole thing was a plan devised by his partner, Max. Max never went to prison. Dad kept him out of the police investigation. On his way to jail, Dad said he'd thrown the money in the river, but Max thinks he hid it away somewhere. Max believes Dad is going for the stashed money."

"How much? Is it worth fifteen years of silence?"

"It's a hundred thousand dollars."

"Not a million, but a nice chunk of change."

"All these years Max has stayed close to my mom, passing himself off as my uncle. She is an only child with no close family so there wasn't anyone around to question it. When Dad was released, Max saw his chances slipping away to get his hands on the money. I guess he figured the easiest way to force Dad to hand it over was to threaten us." Pilar could not hold back a sigh. "He's wrong. If my dad cared about us, he never would have done what he did in the first place." She cleared her throat. "Max caused a head-on collision. The front end of my car was crushed. I was disfigured, and I had plastic surgery to repair my face."

She heard his sharp intake of breath.

She blinked back tears.

"Why?" he half whispered. "Why, didn't you tell me any of this, Pilar?"

The question cut like a knife straight into her. She took a steadying breath. "I'd left, Austin. I made my choice, and I knew what the cost would be."

His fingers whitened on the steering wheel as he stared at the road unrolling before them.

"Anyway, that's three questions," she said with a sniff. "I don't expect your help now. A ride to the first rest stop is what we agreed to, nothing more."

"Come on, Pilar. That's not the only reason you got in the truck," he said. "I don't know you anymore, but there are some things I can still read. You have something to say."

She blinked hard. "I... I thought I might not get the chance again, that maybe God was allowing me this one opportunity. I want you to know I'm sorry...for leaving the way I did."

"Sorry?" he repeated. "Sorry is what you say when you break somebody's coffee cup or lose your temper. Doesn't seem like enough for betraying someone and humiliating them in front of everyone they love."

Her throat closed up and she could not answer. They turned onto the main road, which would take them to the freeway. She could see his jaw working, as he fought through all of the questions her revelations had raised, and the hurt that had come with it. Her lame apology had not helped one iota. It had been a mistake to offer it, but maybe she could at least get some information that might help her mother.

"Now it's my turn for questions," she said, trying for a light tone.

He shook his head. "I don't see why you get to ask anything."

Hard. Bitter. So unlike the Austin she'd known, at least the man she'd known before his climbing accident. "You're right, but I'm asking anyway. How do people arrange adoptions through Sunshine? Are they all Death Valley dogs?" She wasn't sure he would answer, but he finally blew out a breath.

"The animals are from Death Valley and the surrounding areas. Chunk was on our website because he came into the Furnace Falls shelter. The fake adoptee saw him online, no doubt, and called to arrange it. The admin who works in the office assigned it to me because I'm the closest volunteer to the shelter where he was kept after he landed there. I'm the only volunteer in the valley who does long-distance deliveries as a matter of fact."

"Is your picture and name on the website?"

He nodded. "And the information about my delivery duties."

"May I look at the paperwork for the dog?"

He reached under the sun visor and gave her the papers.

"C. Bolt." She gulped in a breath. "I thought it was some sort of weird coincidence when you first asked."

"That name means something to you, I take it."

"Bolt was my father's college nickname. His first name is Cyrus. I wonder how in the world he got my cell phone number." Her nerves fluttered as she scanned the tiny print in the comments section. "There's a typed note at the bottom in the space where the person filling out the form online can add a message. It says 'Artist's Palette' and a date, Monday, five days from now."

"That didn't make sense to me when I read it so I figured it must be a mistake. Why Artist's Palette?" Austin frowned. They'd visited the spectacular cliff formation together, admiring the array of reds, pinks, greens and yellows caused by the oxidation of metals in the rocks.

"And you're supposed to meet whoever sent this there?"

"I think so." She squinted as she read the final words aloud. "'Alone, for Birdie.'" Tears crowded her eyes and her head swam. She closed her eyes and felt Austin's tentative touch on her fingers.

"Deep breath." His voice was not tender but concerned. She was too, gravely.

"I'm supposed to meet him there alone. For my mother's sake. Even though her name is Bernadette, my dad called her Birdie."

"How do you know you can trust your father?"

"I don't. He's a criminal whom I thought was dead until six months ago. When I was ten, he went on a trip and didn't come back. My mom said he'd died of a heart attack. My life changed after that. We moved from place to place, and it was obvious we never had enough money. My mother left early yesterday evening to pick up some craft items. I haven't heard a word from her since. I'm... I'm scared something happened to her. Maybe Max has her."

"You should be talking to the police."

"I called them, but they won't do anything until she's been missing for twenty-four hours." She fingered the paper. "It says to come alone. I'm afraid if I don't, she'll be hurt."

Austin wiped a bead of water from his cheek. "That's the kind of thing the police can—"

"Austin, you don't understand what we've been living through," she snapped. "Max found us, almost killed me. He wants whatever he thinks my father hid. Mom and I talked about asking the police for help, but Max just disappears anytime he wants to." To her dismay, hot tears began to course down her face. "I'm afraid for my mother. I don't know what to do or whom to trust."

Austin pulled onto the freeway, tires

splashing up water. "Let's think it out. Scenario one is your father arranged for this fake pet adoption to get you the message about meeting him. Did he know we were...engaged?"

"My mother might have told him, I guess. I don't know how much contact she had with my father over the years."

"So maybe it was intentional that he arranged this adoption. He knew I would be the one to come. Or it's possible it was coincidence."

After a shaky breath, she swallowed down her tears. "And he didn't want to call my cell phone. Mom said we had to be careful not to talk about Dad in the apartment in case Max had planted a bug. My phone went missing after the accident until I found it in the backyard. I thought I'd dropped it, but I wonder if it was Max and he bugged my phone. Maybe Dad arranged this so you would come and deliver the dog to me in person and I'd read the note." She rubbed her forehead. "This is beginning to sound like some sort of spy movie."

Austin huffed. "Why would your dad take the risk? Surely he'd know a lot of things could have gone wrong."

She shrugged helplessly. "I have no idea. At the least, he knew I would ask to see the paperwork and would read his message. And scenario two is…this is all a trap arranged by Max. But why try to break into my apartment then?" *And where is my mother?*

She stared at her cell phone. She'd turned it off to preserve the battery. Her father, or whoever had sent the fake paperwork, knew her cell number, but had not called it, instead choosing the elaborate subterfuge. Was there really a tracker on her phone? The wisest choice seemed to be to get rid of it, but what if her mother called or texted?

"Here," Austin said, as if reading her

mind. "Use my phone to text your mother. Tell her to reach you via this number until further notice. Be vague about your location. We'll get you a new phone and I'll message if she makes contact."

Gratefully she accepted his phone and sent a text.

Worried. Where are you? Reach me on this phone. Pilar

By the time she'd finished, Austin had pulled off the freeway into a gas station behind a big truck. The driver was inside at the cash register. He pointed to the big mound of garbage bags in the back. "There's a dump not far from here, which is probably where he's headed. Only one way to be certain you aren't being tracked and maybe buy yourself some time."

She hesitated.

"If there is a tracker, it's going to report your location the second you power it on again."

She got out. With fingers gone ice cold, she turned on the phone and tossed it into the back of the truck before she hopped back into Austin's car. Sure enough, in a matter of moments, the truck driver climbed in, pulled out of the gas station, headed for the freeway on-ramp in the opposite direction. If she was being tracked, her pursuer would hopefully wind up at the dump. It wouldn't throw him off forever, though.

"What is your father hoping to get by arranging this secret meeting?" He held up a palm. "I know. I've exceeded my question allotment."

"Doesn't matter," she said gloomily. "I can't answer anyway. Dad is a stranger to me. I don't know how to separate truth from lies anymore." She shouldered her backpack. "I'll get out here. Thanks for your help."

He shook his head. "No way."

"Our agreement…"

"I'm changing the terms of our agreement," he said. "I can't leave you at a gas station in the middle of nowhere. Besides, it will be best for you to stay until we hear from your mom, since she might call at any time. And anyway, if you're stubbornly insisting on going to that meeting at Artist's Palette, you sure aren't going alone."

She saw the determined set of his jaw and wasn't sure whether to be offended or touched at his pronouncement. "You don't owe me anything, Austin."

"No," he said flatly, "I don't. And this isn't because you are Pilar my ex-fiancée." He put a strong emphasis on the *ex*. "I wouldn't let anyone walk into an unknown situation without backup, even my worst enemy. I was taught better."

She knew he classified her right up there as his worst enemy. Situation reversed, he probably would have run too. What did he know of her fear, from his lofty vantage point? Irritation flashed through her. "I had reasons for what I did," she said. "And I don't want your help." All she'd wanted to do was assuage her guilt with an apology.

He shrugged. "We've already established it would be a long journey in the rain."

"I'm not afraid of walking or rain." She reached for the handle.

"Pilar..." He trailed off into a weary sigh. "How about I drive you to Furnace Falls since it seems we're both going that way? At least have the good sense to accept a ride."

Driving rain crackled against the window. If she didn't go with him, she'd have to figure out how to get to Death Valley without a car or cell phone. And what if her mother messaged?

But if she did go with him...

Could she stand sitting next to the man she thought she'd loved with all her heart until it came to a choice between her family and her fiancé?

A long journey?

It might be the longest of her life.

THREE

The drive south through Nevada on Highway 95 was wet and monotonous. An early spring sunset gradually hid anything but the flat road and an occasional peek of mountains revealed by patchy moonlight. The puddle of vanishing yellow light was beautiful, something he and Pilar would both have enthused about in their early dating life. She would say it was the Lord's work, and he would make some funny joke. His mastery of deflection matched her fervent desire to express her faith. He'd been so comfortable with his casual belief in the Lord, until his accident. Then it had seemed that God was missing from the pain and the toil and the hopelessness. Gone when He was most needed. She'd tried to talk about it. He'd shut her down. Wrong, but he couldn't stand to hear her entreating the Lord on his behalf for a healing that did not come.

You and Pilar wouldn't have worked anyway. Better it ended before the marriage began. The ache from his ruined shoulder joined forces with the hammering pain in his temples to obliterate the thought.

He didn't attempt to make conversation, nor did she. The quiet was foreign to him. He was always bursting with things to say, eager for conversation, at least before he'd fallen from that granite peak. Now he could think of nothing to share. *Awkward silence, gotta love it.* At least Chunk's snoring and the jazz music radio station softened the edges as the hours passed by.

They ate the granola bars she'd packed, and she handed him a bottle of water, declining one herself. He wasn't particularly thirsty, but it gave him something to do to keep from peppering her with all the questions he was desperate to ask. The situation was completely surreal. Was he actually sitting next to the woman who'd dumped him, fleeing from some nebulous threat? Or was he dreaming? Maybe any minute now he'd wake up in the small bedroom attached to his carpentry shop with the familiar smell of sawdust that permeated every corner.

"How's your shoulder?"

Her question startled him. "About the same." In spite of months of excruciating physical therapy, and his manic determination to regain his range of motion. He could still not even lift his arm high enough to open the microwave above his stove, but he wasn't about to tell her that. He'd never liked her, or anyone, to see his limitations unless he chose to disclose them.

"Do you want me to take a turn driving?" she asked, when he yawned.

"I'm fine," he said, more severely than

he'd intended. There was a nagging headache building behind his temples. He
cracked the window to see if the chill
air would blast his funk away. It didn't
help and he began to feel light-headed.
Was he getting sick? A ridiculous time to
come down with the flu. Mind over matter, he told himself. If you don't pay any
mind, then it doesn't matter. It was, as his
sister, Willow, pointed out to him often,
an inane philosophy. At the moment, all
he wanted to do was get back to Furnace
Falls, drop Pilar someplace safe, prefer-
ably the police station, and lie down with
an ice pack on his shoulder.

"Gonna stop at this café," he announced,
after another yawn. The clock in his truck
read close to nine, and there had been no
sign of anyone following since they'd left
her apartment. "I need some coffee and
food, and it says they allow dogs. We're
still a couple hours from Furnace Falls."

She climbed out, her clothes not yet
fully dry. His were still clammy too,

but there was nothing to be done about that for either of them. At least the dog seemed in fine form. When he extracted Chunk from the carrier and set him on the ground, he waddled over to sniff her shoes and offered his side for a scratch.

They let Chunk have a potty break on the wet grass under the streetlamp before Austin hoisted him and they entered the café. Red vinyl seats and a country theme with paintings of tractors on the walls made the place feel homey, if slightly run-down. The fluorescent lights stung his eyes. Eye fatigue? He'd been known to drive all night long without ill effect. *Must be getting old, Austin. Maybe this was par for the course at age thirty. Not the same go-getter you were, are you?*

They ordered burgers and coffee. Now that he wasn't driving, his limbs felt downright leaden with fatigue. He hoped some food might revive him. Chunk climbed into Pilar's lap. She stroked his solid, furry body until he sighed with pleasure. "You're such a good traveler, Chunk." He rewarded her with a quick lick to her cheek.

It was the first time Austin could see Pilar in sufficient lighting and he could not keep from staring. He discerned now the scar that crossed her eyebrow, her nose, which was more petite, cheekbones more prominent. Her smile was slightly crooked now too. Under her chin were some remnants of the healing, faint pink marks from the surgery. He might not have recognized her, at a quick glance.

She reddened at his staring. Realizing his rudeness, he directed his attention to the waitress who refilled his coffee cup. After she finished, Pilar asked, "How are the Musketeers?" She was referring to his brood of mismatched mutts. Those dogs had made her the object of their adoration, falling all over each other in their efforts to snag her attention.

"They're as nutty as ever. I guess they'll take to Chunk all right since his adoption fell through. I doubt anyone else will want this old fella. He's got a lung condition, and he snores like a freight train."

"I would take him in a minute, if my circumstances were different," she said. That soft look crept across her face, the one he'd seen so many times before when she was confronted with a homeless animal.

Austin glugged some coffee too fast and burned his mouth. "You always were a softie for flora and fauna."

"Says the man with three dogs at home."

"Yeah. I'm turning into my brother, Levi. He's got a dozen horses, a cat, a dog and a jackrabbit at last count."

She smiled. "Your brother is the quietest guy I ever met."

"That hasn't changed, except now he's engaged. Gonna be married in two weeks as a matter of fact, hopefully before my cousin Beckett's wife, Laney, delivers their baby."

"Really? That's wonderful. Is Levi's fiancée anyone I know?"

Austin drained the coffee cup. "Old childhood friend. Mara Castillo. Almost didn't happen because Mara was nearly murdered back in November."

Pilar gaped. "Murdered? That's terrible. Is she okay?"

"She is now, except for some lasting trauma. They'll work through it together, like couples are supposed to do." He didn't doubt she noted the tone. *Gonna have to get through this*, he reminded himself, *so try to keep your sarcasm under wraps*. What was the matter with him? He rubbed his forehead.

"Are you feeling all right?"

What a question. "Just tired."

She quirked an eyebrow. "For such a committed night owl? You used to say you'd catch up on sleep after you died."

"Guess my body is not on board with my mouth. I'll be all right after a burger."

"Meat, the perfect cure."

He would have thought she was criticizing him, except for the good humor in her slight smile. Losing that smile from his life had hurt like falling off a cliff. And just as he was starting to feel glimmers of acceptance, here she was sitting across the table from him. Only until they reached Furnace Falls, he reassured himself.

They ate quickly and stopped again outside to give Chunk some dog biscuits from Austin's stash and water from Pilar's backpack before they loaded up again. Chunk gobbled up the treats and wagged his tail hopefully at Pilar.

She laughed. "Okay. Maybe just one more, but that's all. We have to keep our svelte pug figure, don't we?"

Chunk took the treat very gently from Pilar's fingers. "You're such a good boy. Maybe you can sit on my lap for a while." She clipped his harness to the seat, climbed in and arranged him on her knees. It couldn't be comfortable for her, really, with the leash draped across her shoulder, but Pilar would no doubt do anything to oblige Chunk. He flashed back to the time when his big oaf of a Labrador jumped out the second-story apartment window above his carpentry shop. Fortunately, Waffles crouched there on the first-floor roof, scared to death, until Pilar squeezed through the pushed away screen and coaxed him back inside. She'd cradled and crooned at him until his shaking stopped. Ancient history, or it might as well be.

Austin stopped any further memories about Pilar and slid behind the wheel.

As they were pulling out, a car entered the lot. A dark sedan.

His mouth went dry. Pilar was checking the vehicle out, as well. It did not come close enough for them to make out the driver, who headed toward the far side of the lot and parked. Austin waited to see if anyone would get out, but he or she didn't. Probably nothing amiss. Checking their texts? Making a phone call? Stopping for a nap? Plenty of innocent reasons.

Pilar was still stroking Chunk, but her face was pale against the cloud of inky hair. Quiet, like she always was, maddeningly so, sometimes.

"Dark sedan. I'm sure there are millions of them in the world," he said. "And I don't see any sign of a lit cigar like the one back at your place."

She snapped him a look. "The driver at my place had a cigar?"

He nodded.

She groaned. "That's proof then, it really was Max. I was holding on to hope that it was some random burglar, casing my apartment."

"You recognize the vehicle?"

Her eyes remained on the sedan. "Max ran a used-car dealership, so he was always driving a different type of car, but lately I've seen a sedan cruising the block.

If I'd have smelled cigar smoke, I would have known for sure."

Austin shook his head. "And all these years you thought he was family?"

She nodded. "He visited every once in a while when I was in elementary school. He vanished from my world when Dad did. Mom told me he moved out of the country because he was sad that Dad was gone." Her tone was bone weary. "How much of my life is an out-and-out lie?"

There was no answer to that. The way her voice broke on the last word made him squirm. So she'd been lied to. It didn't excuse what she'd done, leaving him at the altar like that. He recalled his mother's face pale against the blue silk of her mother-of-the-groom dress, an orchid pinned at the shoulder. Her first child to get married. It must have thrilled her since his brother, Levi, was so painfully shy and sister Willow's relationships always seemed to end in disaster. Their cousin Beckett had still been in jail awaiting trial, falsely accused of murder, and their police officer cousin, Jude, struggling with the investigation, but the wedding had been a wonderful oasis in the middle of that family turmoil. The heartbreak on his mother's face when she'd come to report to him as he struggled with his tie in a back room of the church that Pilar had apparently bolted...he'd never forget it. At least Levi and Willow had each other. He'd always felt slightly outside their "twinness," the youngest of the brood, but with Pilar, he'd been filled up inside, complete.

He had to get Pilar to safety before he started dwelling too much on the past.

As they drove away, he watched out the rearview mirror to see if the car followed. It didn't, or not close enough for them to tell anyway.

As they drove away from the café and out of town, the terrain changed. Rippled hills bordered the road, but none of them very high, like smooth lumps of

clay waiting to be sculpted. The moonlight appeared and disappeared, dancing
with the storm clouds. Light rain turned
to thunderstorms, lashing the high desert.

Austin stayed silent, every crash of
thunder compounding his headache.
Chunk remained sprawled on Pilar's lap,
oblivious to the storm.

"Come on, Chunk. You're quite a solid
doggie. Roll over to the other side, my
knee is falling asleep." She wriggled
him around, but he did not move at all.
"Chunk?" She leaned down, quickly
checking with a palm on his side to see
if he was breathing.

"He okay?" For some reason Austin
could barely get the words out. He shook
his head to clear it. She was staring at the
bottle in the cup holder. "What's wrong?"

"The dog is out cold," she said. "I can't
wake him."

He could not follow her train of thought,
or any thought through the pounding in
his own head.

"You drank a whole bottle of water from my backpack, and I gave him part of another," she said.

"Yeah."

"I order weekly from a grocery store because the water in my apartment tastes terrible. The delivery came early this morning, before I was awake, a case of it on the porch."

He struggled to keep up with her train of thought, but his brain was slow and clumsy. Vaguely he heard her say, "Austin, you need to stop right now," she commanded. "I think there was something in the water."

Something in the water? Like what? "Pilar..." he started, but his words failed, and his brain clicked off into darkness.

Pilar screamed and grabbed the wheel as Austin slumped against the window. She overcorrected and the truck careened off the side of the road, bumping along past rocks that thwacked into the doors.

She fought to stop the truck, but the wheel was alive in her grasp and she could not control it, nor could she get her foot in position to slam on the brake.

"Austin, wake up," she yelled.

He didn't stir.

The darkness made it impossible to orient herself. They hit a slight uphill area as she continued to wrestle the wheel. Hope sprang wild as she thought they might be decelerating. *That's it. We just need to slow down enough that I can guide us.* Slower and slower they went. Austin's legs were blocking her access to the brake pedal. Were they coming to a stop? Finally, she let go of the steering wheel and grabbed Chunk with one hand, fumbling for Austin's seat-belt release with the other. She hadn't managed to find Austin's seat-belt button when the situation changed without warning. In a blink, the truck tipped over a steep decline she had not detected through the curtain of rain. It was all she could do to brace herself against the dashboard, ruing her decision to unfasten Chunk. She held him tight to her chest.

The truck slammed down the slope into the darkness. Tethered by her seat belt, she managed to keep hold of the dog as they jounced and skidded with such violence her teeth rattled. Picking up speed, the truck plowed on. They might plummet off a cliff, or into a ravine. All she could do was hang on and pray.

Without warning they crashed into something, coming to a bone-jarring halt. Window glass cracked with a sound of snapping twigs. The impact wasn't violent enough to enable the airbags, but it cinched the belt tight across her chest and drove the breath from her lungs. The pulse thundered in her throat.

Gradually, her senses began to calm. She allowed a moment to take stock. No blood, no broken bones. She was alive and unharmed. Chunk was limp, but she did not think he had been injured. Fear jangled through her as she unbuckled and turned to look at Austin.

He was perfectly still, but bleeding from a cut on his forehead. For a moment she was completely paralyzed with terror. Was he breathing? She thought she might have detected the warm puff of breath when she placed her cheek next to his mouth. She got out and snatched the dog carrier from the back. Placing Chunk inside the carrier and setting it on the passenger seat, she rushed around to the driver's-side door.

It was buried a few inches in wet, sandy soil, which she scraped away with cupped hands, scooping until her fingernails tore. Tugging did not work at first until she grabbed the handle and yanked for all she was worth. On the third tug, the door reluctantly opened, sending her stumbling back. Austin lay inside hunched and still. Heart in her throat, she put trembling fingers to his neck and felt the soft thud of his pulse.

Thank you, God.

She had to get help. Trying to jostle him as little as possible, she freed the cell phone from his jacket pocket. There was no choice now but to call the police. The phone was locked. She reached for Austin's thumb and rested it on the button. The glow of the screen almost made her weep.

She quickly went for the keypad to dial.

No service.

The sloped sides of the ravine were no doubt interrupting the cell reception. She felt like screaming.

Plan B? Desperately scanning, she was not sure what she should do. The scant moonlight hidden behind dark patches of clouds revealed nothing but a steep slope and a ravine littered with rock and brush. Leave Austin there and hike to the top and see if she could get a call out? Move him out of the way to determine if the truck was still drivable? But she now saw that the front window was a fractured mess and the bumper crumpled. Plus she might hurt him trying to install herself in the driver's seat. The night air felt like a heavy mantle, filled with the promise of more rain. If the storm started up again, Austin and Chunk would be soaking wet in no time. Cold would contribute to shock, and shock could kill them.

"All right, Pilar," she told herself severely, forcing herself to turn away from Austin. "Get moving."

Picking her way over rocks and around prickly cactus, she chose a route up to the top that looked marginally clear. A couple of steps in and the rain began to fall again. She tucked the phone into her jeans pocket and kept going, stumbling and grabbing exposed roots to lever herself up. Water snaked down the back of her shirt. Clashes of thunder swallowed up her screams. Oh, how she detested thunder. In their happier days, Austin relished the chaos, asking her to come stand on the porch of the local restaurant to witness the display; she'd always cringed. Noise and fear were related. Maybe that was why Pilar appreciated the rainbow, but never the storm.

Her T-shirt was soaked, and her breath came in desperate gasps by the time she got up to the road again. Several yards away a drippy cottonwood tree offered the only protection from the rain, so she ran under its spreading limbs and thumbed the phone to life. *Please work. Please. Please.*

No signal.

She felt like screaming and tossing the thing. Instead, she moved a few feet in each direction until she got a single bar. Elated, she prowled through Austin's contacts. His brother Levi's number was first on the list. She tapped out a text, explaining where they were and hit Send. The phone supplied a "loading" message. Hopefully, if she kept walking on the road, she would get a phone signal or at least a spot of good connection that would send the text. It wouldn't hurt to try. She decided to continue on for ten minutes, checking the phone all the while. After that, she'd come back to Austin and Chunk before she figured out what the next plan should be.

A set of headlights appeared in the distance.

Help, she thought with a surge of joy.

Her hand was halfway up in a salute before a flood of paranoia hit her. What if it was Max? There was no one out here to come to her aid if it was. She'd be no match for him if he had a weapon. Alone, vulnerable, easy pickings. Paralysis overcame her, and she drew more deeply into the shadow of the tree.

Should she assume the car driver was someone who could help? Or consider it a possible threat? Advance or retreat? Risk or safety?

Her feet were rooted to the spot. The leaves rustled above as if they were whispering secrets. Trust your instincts, isn't that how the saying went? Her instincts were screaming at her to stay hidden.

But Austin was unconscious, and who knew if he'd been injured by the crash or whatever had been in the water. If she didn't flag down the motorist...

The cost of that decision finally galvanized her. She took one step out from under the shelter of the tree when she saw it...the round glow, too big for a cigarette.

A cigar.

FOUR

Pilar scooted backward under the tree, the branches splattering her with ice cold droplets. She held her breath, praying the sedan would speed off. Instead, it slowed, pulled to the shoulder and stopped, idling. *No, no, no.* She looked for somewhere to run, but there was no cover, save for this solitary tree, and she could not leave Austin unconscious and unprotected anyway. The driver's door creaked open. Her heart hammered her ribs, and it took everything in her not to bolt into the rain-soaked night.

Shoes hit the gritty ground, hard soles, the wingtips Uncle Max always wore. He was always the Dapper Dan, as her mother said. Had there been some sort of hint in her mother's tone that Max was not what he seemed to be? She could not recall. In every encounter he was dressed in slacks and wingtips, a cable-knit sweater in the cold seasons, smelling of cigar smoke and the gel with which he slicked back his gray-streaked black hair. The jolly relative who brought her coloring books and sets of crayons. Good old Uncle Max, or so she'd thought.

Now she watched, stomach flip-flopping, as he stood gazing around, the cigar tip glowing orange in the night. Deeper in the shadow, she covered Austin's phone with her palm and checked again for a signal. Nothing.

Easing down onto her haunches, she searched the wet ground until she found something she could use, an egg-sized stone. She considered. A rock wasn't going to protect her from Max; he was strong and determined and might have a weapon. But it would be enough to buy some time. For what?

Her mind raced. To get back to Austin and pray he'd woken up or find the tire iron or something better than a rock to defend herself with. It was a terrible plan, destined to fail, yet she could think of nothing else, save to run along the road and hope to signal another car on the highway. Also, not a great plan since the weather was bad and it was a remote area to start with. She palmed the stone in her clammy fingers. Scooting under the lowest branches, she eased out of her only shelter, trying to keep to the darkest pockets that defied the watery patches of moonlight.

"On three," she told herself. Her pulse kept time to the counting. *One, two...* She hefted the stone with all her might, aiming across the road to the single spindly tree on the other side. The stone clattered down near enough to the spot she'd intended. She tracked Max's startled movement by the glow of the cigar. Her plan had worked. All she had to do was wait until he crossed the street to investigate. The rain was falling too hard now for her to catch his movements, but she watched his shadow recede as he walked away.

Silently, she cheered. When she could barely make out a silver wisp of cigar smoke, across the road, she prepared to sprint back to Austin. Making as little noise as she could, she slipped and slithered toward the spot where she'd climbed up. Now she noticed there was an easier route down, one that was gentler, covered with sandier soil instead of the root-clogged path she'd used to ascend.

Quickly she scrambled for it, but before she could plunge down the slope, she caught it...that sickly fragrance of aftershave and cigar smoke. Terror swept along her back, drawing her skin into goose bumps. In slow motion she turned, unwilling to confirm what her gut already knew. Sure enough, Uncle Max stood there, smiling that toothy grin.

"Hello, Pilar. Nice diversion throwing

the rock. I used a trick of my own too, left my cigar burning in the crook of that tree and snuck around to follow you. Clever, right?" His eyes drifted over her. "All alone in the middle of nowhere? Good thing Uncle Max is here to help."

Austin figured it was better he'd staggered from the wreckage before he'd emptied the contents of his stomach. The truck was a wreck, but at least there was not that mess added in. His head was still on fire, but he did not feel like the zombie who had awakened a few minutes before to find the truck wrecked, Chunk snoring in his carrier on the ground and Pilar gone.

Where was she? He rubbed a hand through his soaking hair and his palm came away bloody. He was wet and freezing, but on the plus side the cold numbed the ever-present ache in his shoulder. His cell phone was gone, so she'd probably taken it and headed somewhere to get a better signal. Chunk was dry for the moment, but he grabbed a blanket from the wrecked truck and covered the carrier, just in case, before he set out to find Pilar.

The water was drugged? So whoever had done it might have been following. The car that had pulled in at the diner? Now that his brain was working again, he searched the ground near the truck and saw Pilar's small prints leading to a steep ascent. She must have been pretty motivated since she'd always been fearful of the night. By nine o'clock she'd usually be buttoned up at home, a habit he'd never been able to coax her out of.

Could he climb up after her? His shoulder couldn't get any worse. He started up, eager to find Pilar and get her back to the relative safety of the truck. It struck him then that it had been a long time since he'd worried about Pilar. In the past it had been a common occurrence, since she was so quiet often he'd have to guess what she was thinking. *Maybe you talked too much and didn't listen enough.* Had she told him while they were together about the man whom she'd thought was her uncle?

A few paces up the steep trail enabled him to see another, easier path to his right. It sloped more gently upward. He was considering whether to reverse course or stick out the harder climb when he heard a low chuckle.

Not Pilar, a man. Perhaps someone had stopped to help?

He froze, listening intently, but the wind made his eavesdropping worthless. He hauled himself up farther until he could just get a glimpse of the road. Two people, Pilar, the smaller one, and a man. Now he got the scent of cigar smoke too, and his muscles bunched into fists.

Max stood with his back to Austin, talking to Pilar. A car was parked on the shoulder of the road, engine idling. He couldn't see her face clearly, but her body was hunched, arms tight around her middle. He understood the posture. She had nowhere to run, no one to help her. She was completely at Max's mercy.

Think again, buddy.

Austin crept onto the road. It was going to have to be an old-school-style tackle, since he had nothing else on him to use as a weapon. He caught snatches of conversation as he approached.

"I am so sorry about the accident," Max said. "I never meant to hurt you."

"You did hurt me. I had to have my face put back together."

"I'm sorry."

"No, you're not. You want your money. You don't care about me or my mom. Why pretend?"

As Austin readied to spring, a branch cracked under his foot. Max whirled around, the whites of his startled eyes luminous. Without the need for caution, Austin unloaded himself at full speed, a train hurtling out of control.

But Max was too far away. He sprinted

for his car, leaping behind the wheel and gunning the engine. Austin didn't hesitate. He flung himself at the driver's door, yanking at the handle. He almost succeeded in ripping it open, when Max accelerated and Austin's shoulder gave out. He tumbled to the asphalt in a cloud of exhaust, his shoulder screaming at him. Max drove away.

Pilar ran to him.

"Are you okay?" they both said at exactly the same moment.

He exhaled in relief. "Yes. He followed us?"

She nodded, long hair dripping onto his arm as she gave him a hand up.

"I thought I'd distracted him, but I'm not as clever as I'd like to be." She peered into his face so intently. He wished she wouldn't. "The water was drugged."

"Yeah, I gathered that much. I threw it up."

"There's no signal. We've got to…"

Twin headlights scoured the roadway.

He grabbed her wrist. "He's coming back. Run."

They slipped and slid, almost to the edge of the trail when he stopped. She saw it too, the sedan headlights appearing from the opposite direction. Max must have caught sight of the other vehicle, because he immediately swung the car around again and zoomed off.

"Do you have any other enemies I should know about?" Austin said, eyeing the remaining vehicle.

Her brow creased. "I didn't even know Uncle Max was my enemy until six months ago."

"Maybe your father has been tracking us too."

"But he wouldn't hurt…" She closed her mouth, and he knew what she'd been thinking. *My own father wouldn't hurt me.* But she didn't really know her father, and he was a man who'd robbed an armored car and almost killed the guard, so there were no promises where he was concerned. That truth hurt, but better she realize it now.

They scrunched down behind a clump of mesquite, watching the van draw closer. The escape options had not gotten any better with this unknown entity. In fact, they were probably worse. Max might be hunkered down a mile or so away, lights off, waiting for his chance to return.

They listened, tense. Her shoulder was pressed to his and he could feel her shaking, from the cold or fear or both. He put his mouth to the delicate shell of her ear. "If it's trouble, run somewhere and hide."

"What will you do?"

He shrugged. "I don't know yet, but I'm not running."

He thought she might be going to reply when the van stopped, headlights almost blinding them. They heard the sound of a window rolling down.

"Austin? Where are you?"

The baritone bellow made everything inside him relax. "It's my cousin Beckett." They crept out and walked into the glaring lights. Beckett was leaning out the van window.

"Here," Austin called.

Another vehicle pulled in behind him. Austin's older brother, Levi, hopped out, his twin sister, Willow, keeping stride with him. The twins had identical expressions of worry on their faces, though Levi's rusty red hair contrasted with her strawberry blond in the fickle light.

"We got a text while we were helping Beckett with a delivery, so we used the app to track your location." Willow folded her arms. "You know, the app I had to bully you to acquire for just this sort of emergency? What happened?" Willow demanded. She looked from Austin to Pilar, but he saw no sign that she recognized his former fiancée.

Levi was more practical. "Hurt? Where's

the truck? I have a sat phone. I'll call the police. Ambulance?"

"Don't need one," Austin said.

"Yes, you do," Pilar put in. "You were drugged and in an accident."

He regarded her, those heavy lashed eyes, the determined tightening of the jaw, and all the hurt roared back in like a desert storm. "I'm not influenced by your opinion anymore."

He said it in a quiet, easy tone, but he might as well have shouted.

She visibly shrank, hands jammed into her pockets.

Willow's eyes narrowed. "Hold on." She squinted. "Pilar?" She stared from Pilar to Austin, her mouth open. "Please tell me you are not tangled up with this woman again, Austin."

He found himself at a loss for words. How could he explain what he did not understand?

Levi recovered faster than Willow. He

cleared his throat. "Maybe let's not deal with this situation right now."

Even in the gloom he could see Willow exerting all her control not to let loose her true thoughts about encountering Pilar again. A tall order for his impetuous sister. "All right," she said stiffly. "I'm sure this isn't what it looks like. Problem at hand is your truck. Where is it?"

Austin led them down to the wreck where Pilar took charge of Chunk who was beginning to stir. She took him out of the carrier and tucked him inside her jacket for warmth. Levi put the carrier into the van, where they all loaded up to wait for the tow truck.

Beckett didn't say much, which was typical, merely ran his palm over his beard and listened to Austin explain what had happened.

"Drugged?" he finally said.

Pilar nodded.

"Did you call Jude?"

Another cousin, an Inyo County sheriff. "Yes," Willow said. "He's dispatched local PD, and he'll talk to you when he can."

"We'll stay here and keep the scene secure," Levi said. "For now, why don't you two drive back to Furnace Falls with Beckett? The health clinic's still open if you can get him to go, Pilar."

It was strange to hear Pilar's name on his brother's lips. They'd all tried so hard not to mention her after the wedding failure. He couldn't figure out what to say.

"We can't have you sitting here soaking wet," Levi said after a moment. "And Beckett's eager to get back home to Laney."

Beckett shrugged, but he could not hide his pleasure. "Doc thinks it'll be another week or two, but Laney said you can't tell babies what to do. They come when they're good and ready." A rare grin split his face. "'Bout time to have us a kiddo.

She can't get a wink of rest. Says it's like trying to sleep on top of a watermelon."

The avalanche of words and obvious joy lit a spark of happiness and envy in Austin. *Why can't I have that? Couldn't even get my fiancée to stay for the ceremony.* He knew he was deceiving himself. Beckett had almost lost Laney when he went to prison for a crime he didn't commit, and then again when a killer was loose at the Hotsprings Hotel. The fact that they were now going to have a child was beyond incredible, and Beckett knew it. What's more, Beckett thanked God for it every day, as he would tell anyone who asked.

Perhaps Austin wasn't really worthy of God's attention, of His healing. Pilar would disagree, but she could not argue with the fact that He had not granted Austin the healing he'd desperately prayed for. Anyway, at least Beckett and Laney were steeped in the blessings they deserved. And Levi too, with his wedding approaching in a matter of weeks.

"Let's get you two back to civilization," Beckett said. "You're both shivering like kids on Christmas morning."

And with that, Beckett cranked the engine. "All ashore that's going ashore."

Willow and Levi began to exit the vehicle.

"Thanks for bailing us out," Austin said as they slid open the van door. Willow was still searching his face, looking for some indication that he hadn't "taken back up" with the woman who betrayed him. Unable to meet her eye, he looked away. No, not "taken back up," he reassured himself. Just working through this rough patch, as much for his own curiosity as anything.

Still, he felt a sense of relief that Pilar was buckled up, Chunk on her lap. She was safe for the moment, and that meant he could relax.

Relax? With Pilar's criminal father possibly arranging meetings and Uncle Max drugging water bottles? She—no, they—could have been killed.

As he let the van heater ease the shivers away, something inside him stayed cold.

FIVE

The knot in Pilar's stomach tightened as they closed in on their destination. The darkness was almost a living thing, so heavily did it lay over the desert town. Low-lying clouds obscured the brilliant spray of stars. Furnace Falls was the same tiny dot in the massive sprawl of Death Valley, a portal to a past she did not want to reopen. There was a new candy shop, an art store with a Vacant sign in the window, but the town could have been frozen in time since she fled in terror, leaving Austin behind. When they passed the Living Hope Church, she kept her gaze riveted out the front window, not daring to even look at him.

She recalled the anguish, as she'd taken

off the beautiful white dress, which she'd sewn herself. With speed of the essence, she'd left it there, wadded up in a tiny back room of the church. The memory of the fragrant roses in her bouquet was sharp, the handmade ribbon decorations that festooned the end of every pew. Most of all, was the sound of the door closing behind her as she sneaked out. There had been no way out that wouldn't hurt the people she loved. Stay, and she put herself, her mother and Austin at risk from Max. Austin would demand all the facts, and she'd have to tell him everything. Then they'd all be targets. Run, and she'd devastate him, embarrass his family, humiliate herself.

No one understood the cost of her decision to run away…especially not Austin. She didn't blame him, not really. Roles reversed she would not have understood it either. To leave someone at the altar? That was the stuff of movies, not real life.

How she wished it had only been a bad dream.

If she'd had more courage, more faith... A chill enveloped her as she thought for the millionth time that in that moment she'd branded herself a coward, like Austin no doubt thought her to be.

She cuddled Chunk closer, grateful when he swabbed her wrist with his spongy tongue. The effects of the drugged water had worn off without any apparent harm to the old dog. But what could have happened in the accident...she shivered.

They passed the Hotsprings Hotel. Beckett, who had been quiet for the journey, gestured to the old building. "Going to get a new coat of paint on it," he said. "Laney showed me how to put up an online want ad because she thinks I need help. I don't really, but it wasn't worth a disagreement. The siding hasn't been properly painted in ten years, so we're past due. Laney wants a lighter color, says it will modernize the place. Gonna paint the back room too, before Levi and Mara's wedding reception." The enthusiasm in his voice lightened his whole demeanor.

Austin chuckled, the low sound so achingly familiar. It had felt like a lifetime since she'd heard that laugh. She didn't want to admit it to herself, but she'd deeply missed it.

"Laney's gonna drag you out of the dark ages yet, Beckett," he said.

Beckett smiled as he pulled into the police station lot. "If you need a ride later, call me. Gonna go check on Laney. Be up late tinkering on a few things, and I'll have my phone handy." Austin nodded, taking the pet carrier from the van while Laney managed Chunk.

Jude Duke ushered them into his office. His height and build, the square chin, marked him a Duke relation, yet he was a few inches shorter and more broadly built than Austin. Pilar had not spent much time with Jude, only encountered him at some Duke family gatherings, so she was not sure his taciturnity was his nature or if he, too, was hostile toward her for what she'd done to his cousin. Austin filled him in on the facts.

"You two should have stayed and reported to the local PD." He fixed narrowed eyes on Austin. "And you should have gone to the hospital. That was a blockhead move."

Austin lifted a shoulder, his good one. "Won't be my first or last. What do you recommend we do?"

"We?" He raised an eyebrow at Austin. "I recommend Pilar go back to her apartment and sort this out with the police. They'll find her mother. We'll find her father, if he really is in Death Valley and your notion about the whole fake dog adoption holds." He paused. "I read up on the case. Seems like your father has served his prison sentence fair and square, but if he's lying about ditching that money, if he's actually got it stashed somewhere, he'll be headed straight back to jail. Even if he was telling the truth about losing it, he's going to have plenty of debts to pay up on wherever he goes."

"Debts?" Pilar asked.

"The guard. A young guy by the name of Pete Silvers was injured in the course of that robbery, hit by your father when he was driving away."

Pilar sighed. "I read about that when I searched my father's case."

"How badly was he hurt?" Austin asked.

"Recovered from his injuries, but he filed a civil suit against your father. He won a substantial settlement. He collected on twenty thousand of it, your father's savings and the house, but there is still money owed. If ever your father does get an honest job, his wages will be garnished. Could be why he's laying low."

Pilar toyed with the edge of her jacket. "But if he really doesn't know the whereabouts of the money, he won't be arrested, right?"

"Not unless he's keeping quiet, like I said. He's done his time. Sure would like to have a chat with him though. We'll be looking for Max. See if there's something to your story."

Her *story*, emphasis on the second word.

Austin frowned. "She's not telling a story. I didn't just fall asleep driving. There was something in the water."

She tried to ignore the faint spark of comfort she got from Austin's defense.

Jude's expression remained stony. "And if you'd gone to the hospital like a normal person, they could have run a blood panel and proved that for sure."

Austin grimaced.

"What about my mother?" Pilar said. "I can't find her."

Jude tapped a pencil on his immaculate desk. "I can make some inquiries, but we have no crime there. Your mother is an adult, and if she doesn't want to contact you, that's her business. Local cops can treat it like a missing-persons case if you report it."

Pilar understood now. Jude was angry with her, like Willow and probably everyone else in town. He would not step outside what duty demanded for her or her mother.

Austin's phone pinged with an incoming call. "It's Levi. I gotta go make arrangements for the truck to be towed. He's dropping off a loaner. Be right back." He stepped out of Jude's office. Pilar wanted to follow him, but Jude stopped her. She sank back in the chair, cradling Chunk for courage.

"Now that we've got a minute alone," Jude said, "tell me again why you left my cousin at the altar looking like a fool."

Pilar's face went hot. "I found out the truth about my father, and I had reason to believe that Uncle Max was coming to abduct me, and possibly hurt Austin in the process."

"Uh-huh. So you bolted, instead of asking for help."

"I…" She forced out a breath. "I believed I was doing the right thing."

"The right thing," he said, voice low and hard, "is not to bug out on a man who loves you."

Pilar looked back at Jude, his eyes probing hers from under his thick brows.

"You sound like you're speaking from experience," she countered softly. "Who hurt you, Sheriff Duke?"

He sat back. His expression hadn't changed, but she knew she'd hit the mark. He'd endured pain and betrayal, and he would not be able to see her as anything but a fickle woman, like the one who'd hurt him. Plus she'd wounded his cousin, and the Duke clan was tight. She stood. "I'll go back to the apartment and figure out how to find my father myself. It was a mistake coming here." She gathered Chunk and stood.

His gaze locked on hers. "Cutting Aus-

100 Death Valley Double Cross

tin out again now that you've involved him? Why doesn't that surprise me?"

She stopped, throat tight. "I didn't drag Austin into this. I had no idea he was going to show up on my doorstep."

"Maybe it was your daddy who dragged him in this time. Austin showed up, because that's the kind of guy he is. Since that unfortunate mistake, he's been drugged and his truck is wrecked and he's got that look."

"What look?"

Jude paused. "The look that says he has a purpose again."

She was uncertain how to reply.

"Austin's always been restless, reckless even, searching for something he isn't able to identify. Always trying to feed that need with the next adventure, or race or climb or whatever. When you were here, together, he had a fixed point that held him steady."

"I couldn't be his purpose." *Especially after the accident.* "I never was."

Jude was about to reply when Austin returned. "Trucks being towed to…" He broke off, shifting attention between her and Jude. "Did I miss something?" He stepped back as she turned. "Where are you going?"

Pilar didn't answer. She was not sure that she could speak a word without sobbing, and she would not do that in front of Jude. Instead, she pushed by him, ignoring his questions and making for the exit.

Just get away, her gut whispered. *Figure it out yourself. Why did you let him bring you back here?* Jude's taunt stung. Cutting Austin out *again*? Was she? What choice did she have? Cold permeated her body, not merely from the dampness of her clothes. She was practically jogging when she made it out into the parking lot.

She was only a few steps onto the asphalt when Austin stopped her with a hand on her shoulder. "Where are you going?"

"I shouldn't have come back here."

He cocked his head in that way that had always made him look so boyish. "Look. I don't know if it was the right decision either, but it's almost eleven and there's nothing really to be done about it tonight. You can stay at my place. I'll bunk downstairs with the dogs."

Stay at his place. Everything in her went clammy. "No, not necessary. I'll get a room at the Hotsprings."

Austin shook his head. "Pilar, I'm going to be blunt. Beckett won't want you there."

Anger bloomed hot in her rib cage. "Does he think I'm a monster too for leaving you?"

"No. He won't want anyone there who will draw danger near Laney."

Embarrassment burned her cheeks again. "Oh. Right. Of course."

"He's allowed to be ultraprotective. He almost lost her and the baby."

"I understand." She was desperate for him to stop talking. There were no other hotels in town. So where did that leave her? Get a ride back to Cliffton? From whom? She certainly had no friends in Furnace Falls. Call a cab? Travel to nearby Beattie and find accommodations there until she could either track down her father or contact her mother? And what about Uncle Max? No matter what Jude said, he'd drugged the water, she had no doubt. Had he also abducted her mother? The questions pummeled her mind like a vicious spring storm.

"Pilar."

She realized he was staring at her. In the past, he would have swept her along, cheerily persuading her into his way of thinking. He could be dogged in his persistence, so sure his decisions were right. This waiting, the thoughtfulness, was different.

"Just for tonight," she found herself saying.

He nodded. "Fine."

He followed her around to the passenger's side, and she stopped in confusion as he reached to open the door for her. He'd not done much of that in their earlier days.

He noted her surprise and did not meet her eye.

"I don't expect…" she mumbled.

He held up a palm to stop her. "After you left, I…spent some time making lists. Stuff we'd planned on and never did. Ways you and I wouldn't have worked out. Honestly, reasons why I was better off without you."

She swallowed and looked away as he continued.

"Anyway, I guess Beckett got tired of hearing about it so he suggested I should try making a different list of the things I could have done better." He rolled his eyes. "I promised I would to get him off my back." He was looking at his feet now. "It took me a long time to get anything on that list, but he kept at me until I finally started it. Number one thing I wrote down was… I didn't open car doors for you. Bad manners. Too much of a hurry, but that's no excuse."

Her mind reeled. "You don't have to start opening doors for me now."

"Yes, I do." He waited until she climbed in. "Not to restart anything or change stuff between us. To show myself that I can be better." He shrugged. "Or maybe just to keep my promise to Beckett."

So he would be better for another woman in the future, a woman who did not do what she had done.

Swallowing hard, she watched the road unroll before them.

Austin's aching shoulder screamed for a hot shower as they pulled up at his building. This time Pilar practically leaped from the vehicle before he could make it around to open the passenger's door. The carpentry shop was dark, but he could make out three sets of canine eyes, observing him through the window from the shop. "Brace yourself," he advised as he unlocked the door.

Immediately a whirlwind of paws scrabbled the hardwood in a frantic effort to greet the visitors. Waffles, the big black Lab, reached them first. He'd been trained not to jump up on people, but it was clear this new arrival was testing the limits of his self-control. He whined and bonked Pilar's knee with his nose, slathering the hand with which she reached down to greet him.

"Hello, big boy. I missed you. Remember me?"

Austin might be uncomfortable with Pilar on the premises, but the dog was clearly not.

The smaller two animals whipped their skinny tails, big ears swiveling on their wedged heads like desert foxes. They approached with more caution, sniffing at the bundle Pilar held with jelly bean noses. "Hello, Lucy, Ethel. I missed you too. Stolen any more markers lately?"

He smiled at the memory. Lucy, the naughtier of the two, had pilfered Pilar's backpack before one of their excursions, and he did not discover it until she arrived later, her mouth ringed in green ink. Pilar never let him forget it, since he'd panicked, thinking she was ill and running halfway to the truck to speed to the vet's, before she waved the chewed marker at him. Lucy had sported that green tint until her fur finally grew out enough to conceal it.

Austin took Chunk and knelt next to the dogs. They divided their fevered attention between Pilar's petting and the newcomer. Chunk blinked, undergoing a barrage of sniffs, licks, whines and noses stuck in his ears.

"He's our new recruit, dogs," Austin said. "I need to get them some dinner. Way past their time. Then I'll take out the whole gang and we can put them all to bed. You should probably keep Chunk with you upstairs, and I'll have the Musketeers sleep down here in the shop with me."

"I..."

He broke in rapidly, denying her the chance to decline. "That's what we need to do, Pilar.

"I've got my bark-o-lounger down-stairs." The bark-o-lounger was their joke name for the overstuffed sofa in the back of the shop where the dogs hung out when they needed a nap. "I'll slap a sleeping bag on it and bring their cushions down. Perfect solution." He was amazed at the babble that was pouring forth from his mouth, along with the kibble he delivered into three mismatched bowls. There were very few things that made Austin ner-vous. Climbing mountains, scuba diving, starting his own business, even speak-ing in front of a crowd didn't really faze him, yet at the present his stomach was being stampeded by a dozen energetic elephants. Why? Pilar was the one who should feel nervous, right? He shouldn't feel awkward about anything. There was nothing for it but to plow ahead.

He added another pile of kibble on an empty paper plate for Chunk, but the old dog whined when Pilar attempted to put him down. "I think he's a little overwhelmed," Pilar said.

You and me both, dog. "Let's get them outside before we settle him in."

They walked out the rear exit into the grassy field that backed his building. He immediately felt better, an inevitable benefit to being outside. The rain had quit for a while, and the yard was bathed in moonlight, along with the stretch of wild acreage beyond the fence that lost itself into a ravine.

Pilar scanned the space. "I like what you've done with the place," she said.

In a frenzy of business after she'd left him, he'd repaired the sagging wire fence with a new one, added a tree and bench. Another recent addition was a small firepit where he had notions of inviting his family to enjoy some cool winter evening. Thus far, it remained unlit. He'd also built three doghouses. Of course the dogs all piled cheerfully into one...ironically the smallest. The dogs happily did their business and sniffed.

He wouldn't tell her the tree was due to the second item he'd put on his list of things he should have done better... taken advice. He'd stubbornly maintained any tree he shoved into that hard ground would die a speedy death, but botanist Pilar told him many times, "It's a matter of finding the right species for the right environment. There's always a good match."

Too bad it wasn't so simple for people. He watched her gazing at the tree, profile different, her posture different too. She'd been shy, soft-spoken, but confident when she spoke of things that mattered to her. Now she was withdrawn, hands balled into her pockets, shoulders hunched as if she was expecting the storm to start anew any minute. She had changed.

Austin batted away the swell of sympathy. Well, so had he. He'd tried hard to present the happy persona he'd always possessed to the world, but she'd taken that enthusiasm and trampled it.

Again he experienced a flicker of nerves as he led the parade back inside and up the narrow stairs above the shop. The one-room apartment was perfect for him, a tiny bedroom, living area and kitchenette, furnished in sleek and modern grays and blues thanks to his sister, Willow. Pilar and Chunk would be comfortable and safe. There was no way Uncle Max would set foot on the premises without inciting a canine alarm from the Musketeers. If he got past that, he'd have to explain himself to an angry guy with a wrecked truck.

Against her protests, he stripped the bed and put on clean sheets, and found a set of clothes his sister left there when she dog-sat for him, as well as a blanket for Chunk. "There's a pitcher of water in the fridge and some pretzels and bananas, if you get hungry."

"Austin…"

He clenched his jaw. She was no doubt about to tell him to stop fussing, that she didn't want to be there in the first place, that she'd leave at first light, disappearing from Furnace Falls like she'd done six months before. It infuriated him. She had no right to feelings such as those. "It's only for one night," he snapped. "You can stand to be around me that long, can't you?"

She studied him with those silver-gray eyes that hadn't changed, in spite of the upheaval in the rest of their universe. "I was going to say thank you," she said quietly.

"Oh." Heat clawed at his face. "Uh, no problem."

"Yes, it is. I've been a huge problem for

you since you showed up with Chunk, and I'm sorry about it."

He absently scratched Waffles behind the ears. "Yeah, well, I guess this time it isn't your fault."

It was her turn to look away. "It will always be my fault, won't it?"

A tingle floated through his senses. All the things he hadn't done. All the things she had. He was desperate to escape. "I'll let you know if your mom texts." He turned to the door. "See you in the morning."

She did not answer as he left with the dogs, but he felt her gaze on him, heavy. With sorrow? Regret?

He did not turn around lest she see things in his look that he didn't want mirrored back at him.

One night.

You can stand to be around me that long, can't you?

Maybe he'd really meant to ask himself the question.

Could he stand to be around the woman who'd wrecked him?

Quickly he hurried downstairs before his brain started working on an answer.

SIX

He woke in agony, fire spurting through the ruined tendons in his shoulder. The discomfort aggravated him to no end. Bad enough the shoulder was useless, but why did it have to be so painful also? The dogs were a sleeping tangle, all on one cushion, in spite of the fact that he'd laid out one for each of them. Lucy and Ethel cuddled in a ball next to Waffles's belly, all three snoring with gusto. When he sat up with a barely contained groan, Ethel peeled open a concerned eyelid.

"Go back to sleep," he whispered. Because she was approaching age twelve and not one to relish the cool mornings, she gave him a tail wiggle, snuggled in deeper and closed her eyes. In the tiny shop bathroom, he secured a glass of water and a couple of aspirin. He rejected anything stronger because in the past he'd found himself counting the minutes until the next dose, craving the prescription painkillers a little too much. Aspirin would have to do.

It was still not yet sunrise, his cell phone told him, and there were no texts from Pilar's mother or any other messages. Grateful there wasn't a mirror in the cramped bathroom, he did a few stretches, the kind recommended by his physical therapist who had dismissed him with a "we've made all the progress we can until your next surgery."

All the progress…which meant he could still hardly even get dressed, let alone return to climbing. Back in September, a few weeks after the wedding fiasco, he'd told everyone with a jaunty air that he was going to the mountains to scope out some great climbing routes. He'd scoped, all right, and realized with a crushing finality that his climbing days were over. The gear was too heavy for his wrecked arm to heft from the truck. He'd cried. Sat right down there at the foot of Wheeler Peak and bawled like an infant.

But he'd gotten over it, returned to his shop, plastered on a smile to cover his pain and gone on alone. He didn't need a marriage, or climbing, and he'd told God as much in no uncertain terms. If physical impairment was meant to be some kind of a challenge, Austin would meet it, no matter what God threw at him. In his darker moments, though, he had to admit he was permanently scarred, like the cuts that ribboned his shoulder from the surgery. *Quit feeling sorry for yourself. You're past that.*

Or he was, until Pilar had exploded back into his life. She was inextricably linked with pain. The only antidote was to get her what she needed and put as much distance between them as humanly possible.

He shuffled into the hallway to the scent of coffee brewing.

"Austin?" Pilar's whisper floated down from the top of the stairwell. "I heard you moving around. Do you want some coffee?"

Yes, his gut screamed, and his heart echoed with *no*. He didn't want to drink morning coffee with Pilar as if they were friends again. But he desperately needed a hot shower and coffee. Other options? Willow would let him into her place, but he didn't want to endure the interrogation about Pilar that was sure to follow. The Hotsprings was always welcoming, but that was a ten-minute drive, and Beckett was up to his elbows in painting plans and a baby coming. *Man up, Austin.* After a fortifying breath, he trudged up the stairs.

Pilar sat at the tiny table, looking small in Willow's sweatsuit. Chunk still snoozed on the blanket bed she'd made for him atop the mattress. She held the coffee in that way he remembered, one hand wrapped around the mug and the other holding the handle, as if she was afraid someone might take it from her. The coffeepot was full, which set his mouth watering. Coffee first, then shower.

Trying to hide his pain, he poured himself a cup and slugged some down. She was writing something in a little spiral-bound notebook. The memory hit him like a punch. Everywhere they'd gone, she'd had a similar notebook filled with scrawls of her horrendous handwriting, notes about plants, sketches, reminders, Bible verses. How he'd teased her about it.

The words emerged before he could stop them. "Still doing things the old-fashioned way?"

She quirked a half grin, a small scar showing next to her lower lip. "Habits are hard to break. Jotting down everything I know, or think I know, about my father and Max, so I can ask my mother which of them are true." And the flash of pain that settled on her brow made him almost take a step in her direction, arms halfway outstretched to comfort.

Comfort? What was he doing? Old habits, just like she said.

"Gonna take a quick shower." He escaped as fast as he could. Things would be better after the hot water unknotted his muscles and his chin was freshly shaved. But he emerged into the kitchen to find all four dogs circling, wagging, panting and in the midst of it, his cell phone ringing. He waded through the melee and answered.

"Found something when we were out riding, on the edge of my property," Levi said.

"What?"

"A campsite, sort of."

Campsite? Not unusual for spring. Death Valley attracted all sorts of nature lovers. He waited until his brother finished.

"Found a map with Artist's Palette circled."

Now his mouth fell open. Pilar stared at him.

"Real coincidence, being as how you told me it was the place for the meet. Might be your guy, Pilar's father," Levi said. "Then again, could be nothing. Already called Jude. He's coming when he can. Figured you might want to see it." He paused. "Gonna have to ride though. Terrain's too rough for cars."

Austin heard his brother's doubt. His pride poked at him. "I can still handle rough terrain, Levi," he said. "When are you gonna quit babying me?"

Levi didn't answer. He didn't talk at all, most of the time.

"Thanks, man," he said in a softer tone. "I appreciate the info. Be over in a few."

Pilar was watching him as he disconnected. No sense in keeping anything from her. He told her what Levi'd found.

"You could stay here…" he suggested. "I could call Beckett to keep an eye…"

She ignored his suggestion. "I'll fill Chunk's water bowl and fix him a bed on the floor. Probably best to leave him in the apartment, since he hasn't had time to adjust to three other dogs yet. I'll be ready in five."

And that was that. He let Waffles and the smaller dogs out into the yard where they scooted around, excited to greet the rising sun. Pilar joined them and allowed Chunk to get to know his new companions. The old dog seemed more refreshed and relaxed as they examined and sniffed him. It wouldn't be long before he was part of the pack. Matters were simple with dogs. You were in the pack, or you weren't.

Pilar stood back and watched, obviously lost in thought.

"I can go alone," she said. "You shouldn't be involved."

He tried to school the incredulity from his face. "I'm already involved, Pilar."

"But it doesn't have to go any further. I'll get a ride over there and leave for a hotel in Beattie after."

He bristled at the dismissal. "You don't get to tell me where I am, or am not welcome, especially in my own hometown. And haring off on your own is not a good choice."

Her eyes flashed, but her tone stayed soft, as it always was. "I happen to think it is. I appreciate your hospitality, but there is no reason for me to stay any longer."

He'd opened his mouth to pepper her with his exact opinion about her ordering him around like some sort of lackey, when his phone buzzed with a text. He read it, frowning.

"Who is it?"

"A number I don't know." He rattled it off and her face paled.

"It's my mother's cell phone." She hurried to his side, her long black hair tickling his arm as she read from his screen.

Where r u?

Pilar reached for the phone, but he stopped her.

She blinked. "I want to tell her where I am."

"Are you sure this is her?"

Pilar blinked. "But…" Then she stopped, casting him an anguished look.

"Put something in your message so you can tell for sure." He handed her the phone.

After a moment's thought, she texted a message. I'm staying with Cousin Ellen. Where are you? She handed the phone back.

"Let me guess. There is no Cousin Ellen?"

She shook her head. Eagerly she stared at the screen in his hand, but no answer materialized. Her brow furrowed. "Why no reply?"

"Maybe she was distracted, or busy, or driving."

"Or it wasn't her." She bit her lip.

Again he felt the need to comfort, which overrode his earlier irritation. Instead, he stowed his phone firmly in his pocket. "One thing is clear, until we hear from her again, you'll need to stick around, at least until we get you a new cell phone and I can forward you any texts she might send."

Pilar was quiet for such a long time that he thought she hadn't heard. A sigh burst forth from deep within her. "Why do I have a bad feeling about this text? And this campsite your brother found?"

He couldn't answer, because he had exactly the same sort of feeling deep down.

And now there would be no easy separation for the two of them, at least until they got some questions answered.

Before he would have swept her up into

his plans, impatient to do, to fix, to act. He recalled item number three on his list of things he should have done but hadn't. Breathing in so deeply his ribs cracked, he exhaled. "How would you like to handle this?" he said.

Her eyes flew wide. "What?"

"My brother says the campsite is only accessible via horseback. I remember that's not your favorite way to travel. If you'd prefer, you can wait at the main house. I can ride out with Levi and Jude and take pictures for you so you won't have to saddle up."

He thought he saw the shine of a tear in her lashes.

"Thank you," she said, surprising him again.

"For what?"

She shrugged. "Asking."

He forced a grin. "I am trying to work on my asking skills. It's…"

"On your list?" Now a smile crept across

the mouth that was both new to him and tenderly familiar.

"Yes," he said. "Should we talk about what you want to do while we drive?"

She nodded.

"You know, this um, might not be anything helpful. Maybe just false hope." False hope was the worst kind he knew from personal experience. "And there might be some risk involved, if Uncle Max is in town."

She cocked her head in that way he remembered, both thoughtful and teasing. "This pilot I used to know used to tell me that flying isn't dangerous..."

"But crashing is." He finished the quote he'd told her many times. And then, inexplicably, he found himself laughing as they bundled into the borrowed truck.

As they drove toward the Rocking Horse Ranch, he wondered after his whole life had crashed, how he could still laugh with Pilar Jefferson, his runaway bride.

* * *

Pilar had not known Levi and his best friend, Seth, were now running the aged Rocking Horse Ranch. When she'd lived in Furnace Falls, it had practically been an abandoned property. Now the main house was painted, curtains hanging in the window. A curly-haired man with a considerable limp accompanied Levi to meet them.

"This is Seth, Mara's brother. We run the place together," Levi said by way of introductions. Pilar shook Seth's hand, happy to note his wide smile. He was not part of her disgrace, and it seemed like Levi hadn't filled him in on her villainous behavior.

"I saddled up three horses," Seth said. "Jude's already riding over there. Oh, and I saw Beckett in town this morning. He got an answer to his job post for a painter. Guy works cheap too, so he won't need you after all, Levi."

"Good, I got enough to do. Hold down

the fort," Levi said to Seth, "and if that sister of yours phones, tell her I'll call her back soon as I can."

Seth grinned. "It's killing you having her gone, isn't it?"

Levi's cheeks pinkened, but he shrugged. "Only two weeks until the wedding. She's got a lot to plan."

"Like picking out a nice tuxedo for you?" Seth teased.

Levi looked aghast. "Nah. She knows I'd look like an idiot in that." He paused, terror creeping across his face. "Doesn't she?"

"Everyone knows you'd look like an idiot in a tuxedo," Austin told his brother comfortably. He cupped his hands to help Pilar into the saddle, though she knew it probably pained his shoulder.

Swinging up, she took her seat, clutching the saddle horn until she got her balance. *So you're sitting on a two thousand pound animal who could hurl you to the* ground. *No need for concern.* But her fingers were cold with nerves.

Austin swung onto another horse next to her, mouth tight. "This is Patches. You're riding Cookie," he said. "She's sweet as her name. She'll follow Levi's horse, don't worry."

His comforting words made her relax in spite of herself. It reminded her of the Austin she'd known before the accident, the one who wanted her to experience all of the joy and wonder he saw in the natural world, in spite of her timidity. And she had, she thought, as the horses ambled along, heading for a trail cut through the rocky ground, dotted here and there with early wildflowers. With Austin, she'd flown over Death Valley and admired its enormous beauty. She'd climbed rock ledges of canyons and even watched him skydive, though she'd been too scared to try it herself. He had opened up her vision of the world. It pained her that he had lost that ebullience, a slow erosion that started with his injury...and been completed by her desertion.

To calm herself, she inhaled the spring desert air heating slowly in the rising sun. The high was forecast to be ninety, so the sweatshirt would have to go. As it was she was already warm enough to peel it off in favor of the T-shirt underneath, but she was too unsure to risk it while on the trail. They rode down a slope that became increasingly steep, but the horse handled the terrain placidly.

She caught her breath at a large domed shrub with silvery leaves and delicate yellow flowers. The tough little plant was dubbed the velvet turtleback, since it resembled the reptile in shape and the tightly clustered leaves mimicked the look of scales.

Austin caught her staring. "I figured you'd notice that," he said. "That turtle thing, right?"

She was oddly pleased that he'd re-membered. "They're annuals," she said.

"They'll be gone as soon as the weather turns too harsh."

"Quitters," he said.

Was it a joke? Or a jab? She wasn't sure. From her point of view, he was 100 percent dead wrong. Wildflowers were the ultimate survivors, seeds lying dormant, weathering ferocious conditions, poised to seize the God-given moment. She'd tried to express her thoughts during his recovery. *Hardship isn't a test of God's love for you, Austin. He didn't cause your pain, but He's standing there with you through it.*

He hadn't answered, but she had felt it, the simmering anger, the detachment, the despair that he would not allow her to try to ease, the gradual pushing away that opened up a cliff between them. Would she have stayed to weather Max's storm if there hadn't been such a gulf between them?

Her thoughts broke off as the trail continued on in one rough mile after another.

An hour later they picked their way into a hollow, backed by brush-stubbled foothills. In a dip in the landscape was a ragged blue tent. Inside she could make out a bedroll and the glint of a pile of cans. Was this where her father had been holing up?

Levi dismounted, followed by Austin. They tied the horses to a sturdy limb near a rock pile to nose at the weeds. With shaking knees, Pilar slid from the saddle before Austin could give her a hand down. He joined her horse with the others.

"I came across the campsite while I was working with our new horse," Levi said, "getting a feel of her, gauging her comfort on a challenging trail. I like to do that with no distractions, so we rode way out here. Saw this tent and poked my head in. Whoever it is, is living pretty lean. Figured it was some harmless trespasser, until I saw the map with the route to Artist's Palette highlighted. Could be coincidence, since it's a popular place to visit, but it made me think possibly it was your father, Pilar," Levi explained. He frowned as he looked around. "Where's Jude got to? He shoulda been here by now."

"We should wait until he arrives," Austin said.

Austin advocating waiting? He really had changed. Pilar was already closing in on the tent. "Don't worry. I'm not going to touch anything," she called. "I just want to take a peek." Inside the shadowy interior there was not much to see. The bedroll looked as if it had endured many uses. Tucked under the end was the map, a point circled in pencil like the observant Levi had reported. There was a cheap can opener and several cans of soup and raviolis, as well as empty ones tossed into the corner. Was there any sign it was her dad here, hiding from Uncle Max until their Monday meet at Artist's Palette? How would she know anyway? She hadn't seen her father since she was ten years old. He was a stranger, a dangerous one.

She felt Austin next to her. "Anything stand out to you?"

"No. I don't know why I was expecting to find something that would prove it was him. I don't even know him anyway." She shook her head, tears of frustration prickling her lids for no good reason.

He looped an arm around her shoulders, and sighed. "I'm sorry."

A lump in her throat prevented her answering.

And then he'd rested his chin against the crown of her head, and it was so familiar and so terribly sad, that she stumbled away, out of the tent.

"Pilar?" Austin called.

"How did he get here? The person staying in the tent," she babbled. "I mean, it's far away from the road, so maybe he or she backpacked in? Not much gear with them." She noticed an area next to a pile of rocks where the grasses were greener, the desert foliage more lush. The horses were content to be secured there, enjoying the more succulent offerings. Moving closer, she realized that beyond the rock pile and the horses was a depression that probably concealed a trickle of creek when the rains allowed.

The sound of feet crunching over the rocky ground caught her attention. She was about to open her mouth to call for Austin, when a man broke from behind a clump of bushes at a full sprint. He stopped dead when he saw her, mouth dropped open.

His gray hair was long and unkempt. The unshaven cheeks were gaunt. He wore a dirty pair of jeans, boots, a T-shirt with an old tractor on it, and a floppy felt hat. His eyes were an odd pale brown, pale as the rocks underneath his feet. She'd seen those eyes before.

Her mouth would not speak the word until she forced it out.

"Dad!"

SEVEN

At Pilar's exclamation, Austin bolted towards her. Sneaky guy must have been hiding in the brush. There was no way he should be allowed close to Pilar without backup. Austin was still several paces away when he caught movement in the dense bushes behind the tent. What now? Has Jude finally arrived? No. He detected the glint of orange, the silhouette of a gun, but a clunkier model, like the one from the emergency kit on his plane. Fear kicked him in the gut.

"Gun," he shouted.

Too late. The bang almost deafened him. His mind couldn't put the pieces together fast enough as a signal flare sizzled through the air in a plume of spark and light. The cartridge glanced off the rock pile, which changed the trajectory, sending the missile spinning to the earth. Austin's surprise turned to horror as the flare landed in the middle of the horses. Smoke and sparks erupted in all directions; the horses reacted with snorts of terror. Pilar's scream pierced through it all.

Through the haze he saw her on the ground, rolled up in a ball, the tethered horses plunging and rearing all around her. Jude rode up at that moment, immediately sliding from his horse and heading after Levi who was running with his rifle toward the bushes. He had not seen what had happened to Pilar. Only Austin knew she was about to be trampled.

As much as he wanted to assist his brother and cousin, he raced for Pilar. There wasn't time to calm the animals. That would require Levi's touch, and Austin was not as skilled as his brother. He had to get her out from under their hooves. Tearing into the fray, he kicked the flare away into the rocks. It spurted and hissed more sparks as it settled, but the damage could not be undone. The horses were completely spooked.

Levi's horse, Pumpkin Pie, knocked into him and sent him sprawling. Snorts and high-pitched whinnies rang in his ears. He scrambled to his feet and rolled to avoid a kicking hoof. "Pilar," he yelled.

Her hands were over her face as the horses yanked hysterically to be free of their hitchings. Cookie's hoof came rocketing down, directly toward Pilar's legs. Austin gave the horse a stiff-armed shove. He couldn't deflect the big mare, but his action was enough to move the horse slightly. The animal's rear hoof struck Pilar's left shin. She cried out, but he could hardly hear it over the tumult.

He managed to grab the sleeve of her sweatshirt and drag her until he could get her in his arms.

His shoulder almost gave out on him

with the effort. Not now, he told his body savagely. He circled her waist, the wrist of his bad arm pincered in a death grip by his other hand. Head ducked, he pulled her away. As they were almost clear, Pumpkin Pie reared to the side and almost knocked him down again. Teeth gritted, he stood his ground, shielding Pilar as best he could from the blow as he carried her away from the horses. Laying her gently on the ground near the tent, he knelt next to her.

She was crying, her face streaked with tears and dust, still hunched into a protective ball. He saw no blood, but that didn't mean anything. "Pilar, it's all over now, okay? Can you tell me where you're hurt?"

Jude emerged from the bushes and ran over. Levi was ahead of him by several paces, headed straight for his horses, his face a study in fury.

"I'll call for an ambulance, but we'll have to ride her to a place where they can meet us," Jude said. "Not going to be able to get a rig in here, and it's too rugged to land a chopper."

Austin wasn't listening. He was tracking the slight relaxing of Pilar's shudders, the gulped breaths. She was pale as moonlight. Shock? Concussion? "Pilar," he said again. "Tell me where you're injured."

She slowly lowered her hands and sat up. "I... I don't think I'm hurt, not badly." She sucked in a breath. "It's only my shin."

He sought her permission with a look, and she nodded. Easing her pant leg up, he found the mark where Pumpkin Pie's hoof had landed. "Hasn't broken the skin." He touched her shin with the lightest pressure possible. "I don't feel any bones out of place, but you might have a fracture. We should get you to a hospital, in case there are other injuries."

She gulped. "No, I'm okay. Jude, did you find my father?"

"No. I got here and checked out the camp and the surrounding area. I came across an old dirt bike covered in branches down the hill. I was photographing it when I heard the shot. Flare gun?"

Austin confirmed. "Scared the horses."

Pilar looked over Austin's shoulder. Levi had unhitched the horses somehow and let them run into the clearing below the campsite. They had slowed, finally, still trembling, as he talked to them quietly from a distance. Huddled in a group, their ears were pricked, legs stiff. He couldn't hear what Levi was saying to them, but he was confident his horse-whisperer brother would give them what they needed to overcome the trauma.

Jude still fingered his radio. "Be back in a minute. See how you feel when I return, Pilar. Sometimes it takes a while for injuries to surface." He left them to scour the bushes.

Austin wanted to reach for Pilar's hand, but she was cradling her arms around her middle. Instead, he took off the jacket he'd tied around his waist and draped it around her.

She was staring at the horses. "Oh, if any of them were hurt..." Tears welled, and now he could not help himself from reaching out and freeing her hand, taking it in his.

"Horses are way stronger than people, and if any were injured, my brother will know exactly what to do. He's the Pied Piper of equines."

A small smile, his reward.

Jude returned with a flare gun he'd put in a plastic evidence bag. "Common enough, but plenty scary to freak out the horses." He frowned. "Or kill a person if it's aimed right. I've seen some nasty injuries from these things."

Austin stared at the gun. "Who fired the shot? Not Pilar's dad."

Pilar wiped a hand across her eyes. "Max, probably. He can't risk that I'd find out where the money is hidden and claim it before he does. He'd lose out on his prize."

"He could have killed you."

"The only reason he hasn't yet is because he doesn't know where the money is. He almost killed me before in the car wreck." Those silver-gray eyes were stark. It struck him then how many people had betrayed this gentle woman, her father, her mother, the man she thought was her uncle.

And you?

No, he hadn't. Their relationship crash was her fault, surely. Tendrils of guilt twined through his insides. He remembered a particular moment after a grueling physical therapy session when she'd wanted to talk, and he'd wanted anything but.

It's okay to feel not okay, she'd said.

But I am okay. I'm going to get my shoulder back and everything will be the same. He'd read the worry in her eyes.

You don't think I'm going to recover? he'd accused.

I'm praying for that.

God let me fall. I'm going to take care of the healing part myself. Save your prayers. I don't need them. He might just as well have said, *And I don't need you.*

Hadn't he known he was rejecting her on some level as he dealt with his own despair? And what had that felt like for Pilar who kept right on trying, even when he dumped his own disappointment on her? She hadn't deserved what he'd dished out. He willed away the thoughts as Jude finished a quick radio call to cancel the ambulance and rescue crew after he checked again with Pilar.

"First off, are you sure that was your father?" Jude asked.

"Yes."

"Second, did he say anything to you before the shot?"

"No. As a matter of fact, he looked completely surprised. I'm not sure he even realized I am his daughter. I look...different."

"Your facial surgeries, you mean?"

Austin gave his cousin a narrowed glance. Jude could be blunt, too blunt, and he didn't like Pilar.

With a dirty finger, she touched the scar next to her lip and ducked her chin.

She was a little ashamed about her new face, he realized, by her tiny body language tells. His heart cracked open a fraction. Pilar would always be beautiful because her soul shined through with its own light. Her soul did what? His surprise at his own thoughts brought him to his feet when Levi returned. He handed Austin a first-aid kit.

"Managed to get it from Pumpkin's saddle bag."

"Were the horses hurt, Levi?" Pilar asked. Austin activated the ice pack and set it over her pant leg onto the rapidly purpling shin bruise. He used an elastic bandage to wrap it around and hold it in place.

"No," Levi said. "Just badly scared." His brow knitted. "But if I ever get hold of the guy who did this..."

Jude held up a palm. "At least we can confirm it wasn't Pilar's dad. We'll check the flare gun for prints. Might tell us something. I've got my people out looking for Cyrus. He can't go anywhere too fast without the dirt bike, unless that was the shooter's. Two trails to follow now. I'll stay here and keep things secure until more personnel arrives. Why don't you all head back when you feel up to it?"

Levi huffed, arms folded, eyes still on his horses. "I'll leave them alone for another fifteen minutes, before we head back. They should be all right once they settle and I give them a treat." He pulled a handful of half-melted peppermints from his pocket. "Don't leave home without them."

Austin had heard the small gulp, Pilar's,

probably at the thought of having to ride again on an animal that almost crushed her. An idea sprang into his mind. But could she endure being close to him? That close? Could he stand it? Stand it? At the moment, he craved closeness.

You big fool. Don't ride yourself right back into humiliation. She was here to find her father. Period.

And he would help her do that, and that alone.

Period.

Levi led the horses back to the trail, avoiding the area where they had been terrorized. Austin climbed up on Patches. Pilar's knees were shaking.

Such a baby, she mentally chided herself. "You can ride back, just like you rode here," she muttered.

But inside she quaked at the thought of climbing back up on her horse. What if the animal was scared on the way home?

She'd be thrown, trampled? Then she felt Austin's fingers on her arm.

"Scared?"

I'm okay, was on the tip of her tongue. That was the face she presented to the world, quiet, calm, inner fears and disappointments tucked firmly away. But looking into those hazel eyes, something broke loose in her self-control. "Yes. I know I shouldn't be, but I am."

"Someone once told me it's okay not to be okay."

She blinked at him, his white blond hair alight in the late-morning sun. He'd heard her? And remembered? While she struggled with how to respond, he continued.

"Do you... I mean...let's ride double on my horse," he said. "Levi can lead yours. You can swing up into the saddle behind the cantel and hold on. It's a short ride, and we can stop and rest if you need to."

In typical Austin fashion, he'd found a solution to her problem. In his mind there was usually one that shined above all others. He'd plow ahead, try to convince her he was right. "Or, whatever you think would be best for you," he said.

Now she was perplexed. "Okay," she found herself saying.

Levi was agreeable to Austin's plan. "Normally we wouldn't ride double because it can cause lumbar strain for the horse, but Patches is strong and it's a short ride and—" he gave her a look "—you don't weigh much." That last comment made him blush when he realized what he'd said. "Aww, uh, sorry for the personal remark. That's why I don't talk much, usually."

Pilar smiled. "No problem."

Austin kept the horse steady. Levi assisted Pilar to settle into the space behind the cantel, as Austin had proposed. It wasn't too uncomfortable, but as the horse started off, she had no place to hang on, except to wrap her arms around Austin's waist.

The pain of it was like a shot. They'd

had so much joy together, so many promises for the future, until it had all come crashing down. Guilt swamped her. She'd left. She'd run. To protect him, she'd told herself.

Or had it been to protect herself from marrying a man who had become someone she didn't fully know? In either case, she had been a coward. Now, with her arms wrapped around him, and her cheek pressed to his strong back, she prayed that God would allow Austin to heal in his spirit, the place she knew she'd hurt him the most.

EIGHT

Austin made a stop in town where Pilar bought some clothes and a replacement phone to thwart Uncle Max.

"Should I send a message to my mom with my new number?" Pilar's uncertainty didn't have to be spoken aloud. *If that really is my mother who sent the text?*

After a lengthy debate, she decided to hold off until there was a response from her test text. He was relieved. Something about the earlier message plucked a string of uncertainty in his gut.

Back at the shop, he immersed himself in building some shelving Laney had commissioned for the lodge. She was determined to spiff up the place that had not changed much in the last forty years. He was glad the new paint was underway and that he could be a part of the transformation of the Hotsprings. Immersing himself in piles of sawdust allowed him to set aside the disequilibrium he'd experienced since the moment he'd knocked on Pilar's apartment doorstep. Saws and levels, nails and stain, those were normal things that set him back on track. Carpentry required precision, no mental floundering allowed. He sunk himself into the work, surprised to find the hours had flown by.

Jude had asked them to stop by and review some of the notes he'd made for the report about the shooting, so after he cleaned up the shop, he drove them to the station.

They sat in chairs facing Jude's desk, which was cluttered with various files and two half-drunk cups of coffee. While he dutifully filled in the facts he needed, his phone rang. He frowned at the number, gesturing for them both to stay. "Interesting," he answered. "Pete Silvers?"

Silvers? It took him a moment to remember where he'd heard the name.

Pilar obviously recalled it right away. Pete Silvers, the armored car guard driver wounded by her father in the robbery. Jude asked for permission to put him on Speaker, indicating there were others in the office.

Pete agreed. "Nothing I've got to say is a secret. I don't care who hears it."

"What can I do for you, Mr. Silvers?" Jude asked.

"I heard Cyrus is out of prison," Pete said.

"Yes, sir. You heard correctly. He has completed his sentence."

"And I also heard he's in your area."

Jude raised an eyebrow. "How did you come across that information?"

"Total chance. My sister lives in Beattie. She knows all about Max since he was interviewed in the paper after the robbery, the arrogant jerk. She works in a coffee shop. Believe it or not, she saw Cyrus buying a latte and she texted me. So he's there in your area."

Jude shuffled some papers, found a notepad and scrawled something down. "Thank you for the information."

"That's not why I called. His partner, Max—you know about him?"

Pilar's mouth tightened.

"I'm somewhat familiar with the case," Jude said.

"Cops couldn't get enough on him to bring him to trial, but he was the brains, for sure. After Cyrus was convicted, I figured out how they'd both manipulated me and it all fell into place. Max was the setup man. The weeks before the robbery he was watching me, pretending to be a local, friendly. I thought it was a coincidence that he bumped into me at the coffee shop, the gas station, but he was playing me. Figuring out my schedule and routes. What a fool I was."

Pilar sat rigid, listening.

Pete continued. "Max won't be far behind Cyrus. They're both going for the money he stole from the armored car company."

Austin groaned inwardly. The more people who knew about the pot of money hidden somewhere, the more dangerous the hunt became.

"If Cyrus is in Furnace Falls," Jude said carefully, "he has a right to be. He's done his time. Max wasn't charged with a crime, so if he does come to the area there isn't anything I can do but keep an eye on him. If Max or Cyrus break the law…that's a different story."

Austin almost laughed at that one. Max had broken the law, all right, even if they couldn't prove he'd drugged the water bottles and showed up to snatch Pilar.

Pete's aggravated sigh was audible. "This is so completely unfair. I got a pinched nerve from Cyrus hitting me with his car. All I was trying to do was escape. I wasn't even resisting. The injury cost me my job and endless pain, couldn't even take over my pop's business like he meant for me. Now I got some crummy desk job."

Pilar shoved her hands under her thighs and looked at her lap. He knew she felt guilt ridden over what her father had done to an innocent man.

Pete huffed out a breath. "My whole life changed because of those two, and I sure don't want to find out that either one of them got their hands on that money and are living the good life somewhere. That ain't right. They both deserve to be in prison, not on easy street."

"We'll be investigating any criminal activity, Mr. Silvers, you can be sure of that."

He paused. "Could be they're working together, you think? Made some sort of deal to recover the money together and split it?"

Jude's reply was noncommittal, even

though they knew by now that Max was in it for himself.

"I've had a lot of time to think it over," Pete said thoughtfully. "Plenty of time lying on an ice pack trying to ease my back pain, and I remembered something that might help you find Max."

Austin leaned forward.

"What's that?" Jude asked.

"Cigars. That guy stank of cigars every time I saw him. One time outside the coffee shop, he was standing in the parking lot smoking one of those disgusting stogies. We made some small talk about it. He smiled at me and said he got them hand-rolled from a shop in Nevada. The owner smuggled them in from Cuba. Illegal to buy and sell them in the States, so the guy charges extra. Max bragged that he only smoked the finest ones. I figure there can't be too many guys who sell Cuban cigars in Nevada. Figured you could track it down and get his credit card number or something. That might help you catch him, right?"

Jude made another note. "I appreciate the information. May I reach you at this number if I have any questions?"

"Sure."

Jude thanked him.

"Hey, whatever I can do to make sure those two can't get their filthy hands on that money. They don't deserve one red cent of it."

The call ended.

Jude was silent for a moment. "The plot thickens."

"Are you gonna…?" Austin stopped at the look he got from Jude. "Sorry. You'll do your police thing the way you see fit. Call us if you hear more."

Jude was staring at Pilar. "And you'll call, won't you, if your father makes contact? So far he's not done anything criminal that we can prove except trespassing, but I need to have a conversation with him, pronto."

"Yes," Pilar said with a lift of her chin. "My father is a criminal, but I will call you. I know right from wrong."

Austin followed her out to the truck. She was limping from the horse kick, he noticed, so he drove them back to the shop, trying to avoid any unnecessary bumps. Immediately, she headed upstairs. When he'd finished making some shipping arrangements, he found her sitting on the bark-o-lounger with all the dogs nestled around and the laptop he'd provided her with open. Chunk had grown accustomed to his new doggy family, and they were all settled in for an after lunch nap.

He hid a smile. She acted oblivious to the fact that there were four completely contented canine companions sharing her couch. "What are you researching?"

"My father's case. It bothers me that I didn't know he hurt that guard until I read up on it myself. Mom kept that part from me, among other things, when she finally did tell me about what happened. I was trying to find out more about Pete Silvers too."

"Why does that matter?"

"I'm not sure, except to reassure myself that he really did recover somewhat from what my father did to him." She sighed. "From what I can tell, Pete is doing better than I am. He works in the office of his father's contracting business in Southern California."

"Could he be involved in what's happened lately? Made up the whole story he told Jude?"

She considered, the quirk of her eyebrow so familiar it made his chest tightened for a moment. "He has a right to a grudge, I guess, but even if the money was recovered by the police, Pete wouldn't get any of it, I don't think."

"When your father was arrested, where exactly did he tell police he'd tossed the cash?"

"That's the other thing I've been looking into. He apparently told them he panicked and chucked the duffel bag into a river on his way out of Las Vegas. The police dragged it, but never found anything."

"Another lie?"

She sighed. "Max must think so. He figured my father would get out of prison eventually and retrieve it, but that won't help Pete Silvers."

"Right," Austin agreed. "He won't get a cut of it anyway, since it's not your father's in the first place."

"I suppose he will get satisfaction of seeing them punished, if they're caught." She frowned. "Max's primary goal is to take the money and disappear before my father can."

And he doesn't care about who he has to kill to get to it first, Austin refrained from adding. The sound of the trampling hooves replayed in his memory. Pilar trapped. *She's not helpless,* he reminded himself. And she was plenty determined enough to walk out on him without a backward glance.

He still felt unsettled from their wild morning. Not so much from the incident with the flare gun, he realized, as from the feel of her arms around him as they rode. And the vulnerability she'd expressed about being afraid to ride. The admission was not her typical quiet deflection. Pilar was different, and the change intrigued him as much as he didn't want to acknowledge it.

Busying himself, he checked his phone again. Still no messages. He was filling a cup from the shop watercooler, when there was an explosive knock on the front door. The handle rattled and another knock came.

Pilar looked up in fright.

He gestured for her to stay back as he crept to the window, grabbing a baseball bat he kept in the umbrella stand near the threshold. Creeping closer, he lifted the shade enough to see out. Exhaling in relief, he unbolted the door for Beckett.

"Why'd you lock the door?" Beckett panted. "You never do that."

Austin arched an eyebrow. "I dunno, people drugging me and wrecking my truck, shootings… Seemed like a good idea."

The sarcasm bounced right off Beckett. That and his lack of inquiry about the shooting made Austin realize he was distraught. "What's wrong?"

Pilar put aside the laptop, eased out from the pile of dogs, and joined him.

Beckett fisted his hands on his hips and took a breath. "It's Laney."

"What?" Austin said, instantly swamped with concern. "What happened?"

Beckett's mouth was tight with uncharacteristic emotion. "She got dizzy this morning and fell in the hotel kitchen. Doc says her blood pressure is spiking." He rubbed a calloused palm over his stubbled chin. "She's okay, but panic-stricken,

even though the doc said the baby is unharmed. It took me forever to get her to
believe it. Doc's put her on bed rest. I
got her staying with Aunt Kitty because
she's gonna be stressed at the Hotsprings
watching all that needs to be done and not
being able to help. Plus when we paint
the back area, it might make some fumes
and I'm not going to have her around that.
I brought Admiral along, and he's some
comfort." Laney did not go anywhere
without Admiral, her aged, one-eyed dog.

Beckett looked from Austin to Pilar to
the dogs and back again without apparently seeing any of it.

"What can we do?" Pilar asked, taking
the words right out of Austin's mouth.
"How can we help?"

"Anything," Austin echoed. "I can help
with the painting." As soon as he said it,
he wondered how in the world his shoulder would tolerate the abuse. Grimly, he
decided he would hold the paintbrush in
his teeth, in order to help Beckett and

Laney. More pressing was how to arrange protection for Pilar.

Beckett shoved his hands in his pockets. He was not a man accustomed to asking for help. Austin forced himself to be quiet, to allow Beckett to say what he needed to in his own time.

"Willow's at the hotel now, giving Herm a hand with the cooking for the next few days, just to get through the weekend. I can handle the tours and guest check-ins and -outs, but..."

"But what?" Austin hated to see Beckett in torment.

"We got this big group staying at the hotel right now, part of a spring wildflower tour, thirty-two people. With that large a group, plus a dozen other families, the dinner service is killing me. Plus I gotta stay on the painting project during that time so we can get the lodge exterior wrapped up by the weekend. I'd cancel the painter, but I already stripped and sanded the back, so I gotta get it done before the next storm comes in. Plus we have Levi and Mara's wedding reception there, and Laney said that was to go forward no matter what or she would throw a fit the likes of which I'd never forget." He chuckled.

"I believe it," Austin said.

Beckett's faint smile dimmed. "Truth is, we really need some traction at the hotel. It's been so long since we had any good traffic. Don't feel like we can withstand bad reviews if the guests aren't happy."

The hotel had been nearly deserted the past two years when Beckett was in prison, accused of murdering a woman on the property. When another woman was murdered after his release, things had gone from bad to worse until the killer was finally caught. The Hotsprings needed bad publicity like a carpenter needed termites. He was going to jump in when Beckett started up again.

"I don't like to ask you since you got everything going on..." he said.

"You're not asking," Austin said. "I'm offering. I'll help with dinner service." He flashed a grin. "And I won't even demand tips."

"I will too. I have waitressing experience." Pilar's expression grew tentative. "I mean, if you don't mind me being there and such. I understand if you're not comfortable."

Beckett heaved out a breath. "Laney is all buttoned-up safe at Aunt Kitty's. Don't think it would be any harm in you two pitching in for the dinner service for a couple of days until I can get some temporary workers."

Austin relaxed. It was the perfect idea, really. He could think of no safer place than the Hotsprings, full of guests. Plus Pilar would not escape his watchful eye for a moment. Maybe they could even pick up some sort of hint about strangers in town. "All right. It's done then. What time should we report for duty?"

Beckett's smile was weary, but hopeful. "Four would be great. I owe you both, big-time."

Austin laughed. "You can pay us in cake at Levi and Mara's wedding reception...or maybe with those tiny finger sandwiches when we have the 'You're a Daddy' party."

That got another chuckle from Beckett. "Done. I really appreciate it."

As Austin saw him out, he still detected the grooves of worry on Beckett's forehead. Not about the hotel, he knew— about his "one and only," as he called Laney. That pair had weathered an unbelievably ferocious storm, and their love had come out stronger for it. It was the only reason Austin had started that dratted list. Beckett was his hero in more ways than one.

"So what's your guess?" he asked Beckett. "Is Laney going to have a boy or girl?

That stopped Beckett and the transformation on his face awakened an ache inside Austin for some reason he did not understand.

"Laney thinks it's a girl on account of some such thing Aunt Kitty told her about the shape of her belly."

"But you want a boy?"

And then he looked Austin dead in the face with such a fervent expression that it stopped Austin cold. "I could have lost everything, because of my pride. Instead, I got grace." He shook his head. "I trust Him with whichever He brings into our lives." And then he was jogging to his truck.

I could have lost everything, because of my pride. The words struck a melancholy chord in Austin until a buzz on his phone snapped him back. He relocked the door.

"I got a text message, Pilar."

Pilar hurried to peer at the screen.

There is no Cousin Ellen. Will call you tonight at seven. It's urgent.

Joy broke over Pilar's face. "It's my mom. She's okay. Let's text her my new number."

She'll leave, was his unfiltered thought. If Pilar's mother did not need to contact her through Austin's phone, Pilar would be free to go. No, he reassured himself. She'd agreed to help at the Hotsprings for a few nights, and she would never break a promise like that. His second thought was a concern that he'd finally lost his mind for good and all.

He was upset that Pilar might leave? What was his problem? She was not his friend, not his fiancée anymore, and until two days ago, he'd actively despised her. Now he didn't want her to go? What madness was this?

She touched his arm. "What's wrong?"

He rallied a smile. "Nothing. Glad your mom is okay."

Her slight frown said she didn't buy it. It was that ability that got to him, her skill in poking right through his facade. Post-injury, it had become intolerable, that she could see what he didn't want her to, the insecurity, the pain, the hopelessness. He wanted to show only the curated parts where he was a whole man, confident, capable, and it grew increasingly impossible for him to do that in front of the one person he could not fool.

He detached himself from her. "I'm going to finish up a few things in the shop while you send the text." He walked away before she could say anything more, but he had the feeling that she was searching for the truth in him.

I won't let you have the power anymore, Pilar.

Pilar slipped on her purchased jeans and T-shirt and grabbed a small pouch. Austin hadn't wanted lunch, so she'd eaten a peanut butter and jelly sandwich by herself in the apartment. She peeked out the bedroom window into the yard below. The dogs were all situated, soaking up the afternoon sun. Chunk was comfortable now too. They'd set up a cushion just for him in his own private doghouse where he could find shade and water if he didn't want to consort with his younger companions. At present he seemed delighted to hang out with his new pack.

Levi had delivered Austin's repaired truck, so they drove to the Hotsprings a few minutes before four. Austin was quiet, and she felt he had his defenses up about something, but she couldn't tell what. *Not your concern, Pilar.* The time was growing short until she would be able to talk to her mother. Once she knew her mom was safe, they could figure out what to do about her father. What a family tree. She was not worried about Max getting close to her at the Hotsprings, since she would be fully occupied in a jammed dining room and kitchen the whole evening.

True enough, they arrived to find the lodge bustling with dozens of visitors arriving for the early dinner hour. Afterward, Austin told her, Willow would lead a caravan of eager photographers to witness the glorious spring sunset, and drive in Death Valley National Park for a night star viewing.

There was a faint whiff of paint in the air as they parked and let themselves in the back, but not enough to be off-putting to the guests. She followed Austin into the kitchen, where she found Willow mixing an enormous bowl of salad.

"Hi, Austin," she said. "Glad you're..." And then her gaze settled on Pilar. "What...?" she started.

"She's helping serve dinner," Austin said. His tone held a warning. *Don't make a big deal about it*, most likely.

Willow shook her head and heaved out a breath. "Okay. I'm a team player. Pilar, this is Herm, the cook."

Herm waved a slotted spoon at her. "How do?" His bushy white eyebrows were arched in a look of mild surprise.

He must have heard about her flight from Furnace Falls. Who hadn't? He plunged the spoon into a fragrant pot of baked beans, signaling the end of the chitchat.

"Can you two get these salad bowls to the buffet?" Willow said. "Dressing's already out there. Herm's about ready to carve the brisket, and the platters of chicken are in the oven to keep warm." She ticked off the items with a plastic gloved hand. "Meat, biscuits, salad, beans, lemonade, coffee and water. That will do until the dessert course. Can you handle it?"

"Yes, ma'am," Austin answered for them both. "But aren't you supposed to be babysitting your imaginary friend's kids?"

Pilar knew Tony was a pilot friend of Willow's whom Austin nor Levi had yet to meet.

"He's got someone else to watch them. I'll see him later."

Pilar and Austin set their windbreakers

on a side table, and she added her pouch. Gathering up an enormous bowl of salad, she marched into the dining room. The guests were not shy, nor were they suffering from a lack of appetite. She was glad for the frantic pace, which allowed her to keep from trying to make strained conversation with Willow on her trips back to the kitchen. Clad in denim aprons with Hotsprings embroidered on the front, they raced back and forth, filling and refilling, answering questions and wiping up spills. Beckett checked in to make sure things were running smoothly. He looked more focused and less panic-stricken.

Austin kept scanning the guests and the bank of windows for any sign of Max, but there was none. The crowd made a respectable dent in the mountains of food, which then had to be cleared for the dessert service. Her nose identified the chocolate cake and fresh churned ice cream before she clapped eyes on it. Buckets of ice cream and platters of cake had to be moved from kitchen to dining room and served up.

Before Austin could get to the ice cream scoop, she snatched it up, leaving him to dole out slices of cake. She knew his shoulder was not up to the task. If he'd figured out her plan was to save him discomfort, he didn't show it, handing out cake slices with a wide smile and friendly banter. When the service was finally over, they reported to the kitchen to help with the dishes.

Herm insisted they sit outside at a tiny courtyard table to eat platefuls of food he'd served up.

"Sit with us," Austin said to Willow, and Pilar thought there might be a pleading note in his voice.

Willow arched a frosty eyebrow at Pilar. "Nope, I have a tour to lead. See you tomorrow, same bat time, same bat channel," she sang out as she left.

Pilar checked the time. "Almost five.

Two more hours until Mom will message."

They dug into their meals. The slow-cooked brisket was fragrant with garlic and herbs. It had been a long time since she'd enjoyed a well-cooked dinner. She was forking up her last bite when a man in paint-splattered overalls exited the kitchen, holding a paper plate full of cake.

"Oh, hey," he said. "Herm said to tell you he's got your desserts inside."

"Thanks," Austin said. "You must be the painter."

"Yeah. Name's Gary."

Austin introduced them. "Appreciate you stepping in to fix up the place. Especially with so much going on."

He winced. "Always good to get work, but I'm remembering why I need to get out of the painting business." He raised an eyebrow. "Hey, uh, I guess I'm nosy by nature, but I heard in town there was a trespasser on the horse ranch. That was you two involved with that, huh?" He lowered his voice. "Is it true that old robber who got out of prison has a stash of money hidden somewhere here and he's come to claim it?"

Pilar's throat tightened. What would Gary say if he knew he was speaking to the old robber's daughter? She was glad for the first time her face was altered. There might be a family resemblance some savvy local might notice from the newspaper pictures that she'd discovered in her computer sleuthing. Her father's crime had been front page news in Las Vegas where they'd lived at the time, and it had no doubt grabbed the attention of Death Valley residents as well. It explained why her mother insisted they use her maiden name, Jefferson, when they moved to Parumph where they'd lived until Pilar came to the Death Valley area for her botany studies. Funny how she'd never questioned why she didn't have her father's last name.

Mom, why couldn't you have told me the truth? Their scheduled evening phone call would only scratch the surface of the million questions popping up like weasels.

Gary was staring while trying to appear not to do so. She shrank in upon herself. The only thing that traveled faster than lightning in a small town was rumor. She wondered who was spreading the news.

"Sounds like gossip to me," Austin said, voice clipped. "What business is that of yours? Are you hoping to find a stash if there is one?"

Gary laughed. "When I have this lucrative painting business? No time for that, but there were plenty of people soaking up the conversation. This one guy in particular." Gary shook his head. "That guy had to have been from out of town."

Pilar felt a quiver. "What guy?"

"Dunno him. I haven't been here very long myself, you know, but I thought it was weird, is all. He practically bumped into me and I almost spilled my latte. He split when a cop came in."

Austin eased into a more friendly tone. "Yeah? What did he look like?"

"Short, dressed in nice shoes, mustache. That's why I thought he had to be a stranger. No local wears fancy shoes, right?"

Pilar's heart sank. "Did you happen to hear where he was headed? Any indication of where he might be going?"

"Nah, didn't catch him speak at all, but he sure looked like he had a mission on his mind when he left."

Austin's friendly nod was at odds with the tension in his body.

A mission to kill, she thought with a shiver.

Gary sauntered off to eat his cake in solitude.

Austin was looking out at the road that passed the long Hotsprings driveway.

She heard his sharp intake of breath as her eyes found the source of his concern. A sedan driving slowly along.

NINE

The sedan passed. Was it Max's? Too far away to get the license plate. There had to be more than one dark sedan in Furnace Falls. Austin hurried Pilar to pack up and leave immediately for the safety of the shop. Suddenly the beautiful Hotsprings vistas felt very wide open.

Pilar gathered her things from inside along with Austin's windbreaker and they hit the road. He scanned in both directions but saw no sign of the sedan. Max couldn't have known they'd be helping out at the hotel, could he?

Austin dutifully called Jude from the truck and told him about Gary's comments and the sedan sighting.

"I'll circulate a picture of Max to all

the local shop owners," he said. "He can't hide long in a town of a thousand people."

Austin wasn't satisfied, but he didn't figure there was much else they could do. Infuriating that Max could waltz around while Pilar had to be imprisoned.

Pilar fiddled and squirmed in the passenger seat, repeatedly checking the dashboard clock...nearly half-past six. Plenty of time before Pilar's mother called. Hopefully. He let them into the shop.

"Dogs will be ready for their supper for sure," he said, going to the back door to usher them in from the yard. He flipped on the porch light, unlocked the bolt and stepped into the yard. Immediately, the silence put him on full alert.

"Dogs?" he called.

No answering canine chorus. Nothing, except for one pitiful whine. The hairs on his arms lifted. Why didn't the animals greet him with their usual slobbery chaos?

Pilar was behind him in a moment. "What's going on?"

Prickles erupted on the back of his neck. "Go back inside, Pilar. Something's wrong."

He returned to the shop long enough to grab the bat before he charged out into the night.

The darkness was complete except for a frail arc of moonlight. "Dogs!" he shouted again. There was no frenetic barking from the Musketeers. In a moment, he found out why. Their doghouses were empty. It took him another few minutes to decipher what had happened.

There was a four-foot hole cut in the wire fence. Chunk stood in the dark shadows outside the hole, mourning the loss of his companions. "It's okay, boy. I'm here."

Austin found the metal pole, scratched and dented where it had been whacked against the fence to terrify the animals. That explained why the dogs hadn't gone back to their yard. They'd been spooked into running away, all except the elderly member of the pack that couldn't keep up with them.

His nerves exploded. He ducked through the hole, scooping up Chunk. He was shaking and his tongue lolled, but otherwise appeared unharmed. "Waffles," he yelled. "Lucy, Ethel." The only answer was the swishing of the grass in the spring breeze.

Pilar called from the porch. "The fence is cut?"

Fury spiraled through him in a white-hot surge. No one would mistreat his dogs and get away with it. He stormed back to the house, bundling Chunk into her arms. "Keep the door locked and call Jude."

"Where are you going?" she called after him.

But he would not stop. At the front curb, Pilar tried to grab his sleeve. "Austin, you shouldn't go out there alone."

He pulled away, teeth ground together,

pulse slamming through him. "I'm going to find my dogs and whoever took them."

He gunned the engine and shot down the road. One turn, a second, took him to a fire trail cut through the wildland. Then he was jouncing along the graveled road, thoughts whirling. Those misfit mutts were his family, the ones who heard him crying, ranting, after Pilar left. They'd soothed him when pain kept him pacing the floors. They'd been there when the nights were endless and it felt like the mornings would never come. They were his family. The more he'd shut God out, the more he talked to the dogs. A terrible well of desperation blackened his vision.

But maybe, just maybe, it was possible that God still heard him too.

"Lord, my dogs don't deserve to be hurt. Please..." He was ashamed when his voice broke. *Get it together, Austin. You're the one behind the wheel. Find the dogs yourself.* Fury stoked higher, he accelerated until the truck was rattling over dips and holes, pinging rocks under the chassis. After about a mile with no sign of them, he left the trail, hoping his four-wheel-drive vehicle would stand up to the punishment. He plunged deeper into the unkempt land, miles of snarled grass, boulder piles and shrubbery, stopping only when he came to the deep, rocky ravine.

When he'd first started the shop, he'd spend his free time there, exploring the deep gouge in the earth, home to coyotes, snakes and mountain lions. Predators. His pulse pounded against his throat. The wilderness of Death Valley was no docile beast. In such a harsh climate, only the most tenacious survived. Waffles was a brave protector for the smaller dogs, but he wouldn't hold up very long against a hungry coyote or mountain lion on their home turf. The natural enemies were deadly…and so were the unnatural ones.

Someone had set his dogs loose, scared them badly enough that they'd run.

Not someone. Max.

Fearful that he'd blow a tire on the sharp rocks, he jammed the truck into Park and got out.

"Dogs," he yelled so loudly his voice echoed and bounced along the ground and down into the canyon before it was tossed back up to him again. Surely if they were close, he'd hear an answering bark…if they were still alive. He hollered again.

This time, he got an answer, a deep woof that sent joy firing through his nerves. He'd know that bark anywhere. Waffles.

"Come here, boy," he yelled as loud as he could. At first there was no movement from the dark ravine beyond. Then all at once, Waffles came galloping into view, Lucy at his heels. They ran to him and he dropped to his knees to accept their slobbers. If dogs could cry, he knew, their eyes would be as wet as his were. He clutched their trembling bodies close for a moment. "Everybody okay? No cuts or broken bones?" As best as he could tell with his flashlight, they were in perfect health.

He looked beyond them. "Where's Ethel?"

The dogs clamored in confusion, following as he set off. He scoured the direction they'd come from, searching under rocks and through grasses, praying the rattlesnakes were asleep for the night, but there was no sign of Ethel.

Had she been injured? Eaten? Did Max take her?

"Lucy, where is Ethel?" he demanded of the small dog, only to receive an anguished whine in reply. He'd search, comb every corner of the ravine. Ethel might be injured, lying in pain, afraid to be alone. He was halfway down to the ravine when he stopped suddenly as the word hit him.

Alone. His blood turned icy.

He'd taken the bait.

He'd left Pilar alone.

Pilar had dutifully taken Chunk back to the house, locked the front door and called Jude who promised to be over immediately. When she put Chunk down, he yelped and she saw to her horror, he'd dripped blood on the floor. She traced the source to small cut on his side.

"Oh, you poor sweetie." She fetched a cotton ball from the shop bathroom and hoisted him over the sink to clean the wound. "It's only a tiny cut. That's a relief."

It wasn't until Chunk's ears swiveled at some faraway sound that it occurred to her she'd been so flustered she hadn't engaged the wooden bar at the back door, the one Austin had cut as a secondary security measure. Extra caution couldn't hurt, especially now.

She set Chunk gently down and was

a few steps away from the back door when it opened. Max stepped into the shop, pocketing a lock-picking tool. He was wearing a black slouch hat and was clothed completely in black all the way down to his wingtips. He must have been hiding in the woods, hoping Austin would go chasing after his dogs. He'd laid a trap, and this time she'd been caught. Fear chilled her limbs.

"Get out of here," she said.

Max pulled a gun from his pocket. "I don't think so."

She bit her lip to keep from screaming as he gestured for her to sit on the bark-o-lounger. Mouth dry as sand, she sank down. Chunk pattered over and cowered at her ankles. *Run*, she wanted to tell him. *Run away from this bad man.* "You let the dogs loose?" she said finally, over her pounding heart.

"I had to talk to you," he said. "Couldn't figure a better way." His eyes were shadowed, and he did not sport his ever-present cheeky grin. "Where is he?"

"Who?"

She heard his teeth grind. "Pilar, I don't have time for this. I expect your ex-beau to be back shortly. Your father contacted you. That's why you came to Furnace Falls, to meet him."

"You drugged the bottled water, didn't you? Why?"

He grunted. "Poison isn't my style."

"You prefer guns? You could have killed me with that flare gun."

His eyes narrowed. "Quit being dramatic. It's not going to work to stall. Give me what I want, and you'll never see me again. I promise."

"Your promises don't mean much. Did you promise my father you'd help him with the holdup? That worked out well for you. You didn't even do a day of jail time and he went to prison."

"Don't get it mixed up. Your father is no kind of a tragic hero," Max said with a sneer. "He took the money and hid it from me, his partner."

"Some partner."

"It's mine," he said savagely. "It was my plan. I did all the research. Learned the new guard's route. Had it timed down to the minute, except the guy got loose and ran for the cops, which is why your dad hit him. Couldn't even do that right because the guard lived to identify him."

"And you were safely parked two miles away."

He tamped down his mustache with the hand that wasn't holding the gun. "I was waiting at our rendezvous spot, keeping watch for the cops, but your daddy dearest decided to double-cross me after he messed up the plan. Three days later when they caught him, there's no money. He comes up with that 'chucked it in the river' story. I didn't believe it for a minute."

"Yet you were happy to let him do the prison sentence without coming forward to admit your part in it. And Dad never spoke out against you, did he? Told everyone he'd planned it himself."

"The cops didn't believe him. There just wasn't enough evidence to pin me for it. Look," he said. "I don't particularly want to kill you, but I need my money. You won't be able to keep it for yourself, if your dad tells you where it is before I get there. I'll hound your every step until the day you die."

"I don't care about the money."

He smiled. "Honey, everyone cares about money, and if they don't, they're liars. All my life I've scraped by, and that job was my ticket out of the rat race."

"Everyone scrapes by," she said, throwing his words back at him. "You made choices and you have to live with them. You could have been an orthodontist instead of a robber, couldn't you?" Her own boldness startled her.

"Shut up," he snarled. "You sound like my old man. Worked hard for a paper mill all his life and what was his reward? No savings and a heart attack at age sixty. I'm not going that route. I'm taking what's mine while I can."

How long would it take Jude to arrive? How much time had passed since her call? She wasn't sure. And anyway, Jude had no idea Max was two feet away from her so he might not be coming with lights and sirens. As for Austin, who knew how far he'd had to go to find the missing dogs. Stalling. That was the only answer that presented itself in her panicked brain. "The money is your business, and I don't care about your grudge with my father. You two can work it out. I just want my mom safe."

He cocked his head. "Is she missing?"

Pilar detected something in Max's expression. Was he trying to cover up guilt? Surprise? Or worry? Did he know something about her mother? If this was a game of cat and mouse, she was not sure which animal she represented. *Sneaky* was not in her wheelhouse. "I don't know," she said finally. "Do you?"

He was silent for a long moment. "No more evasions. Tell me where your father is, Pilar. I'm running out of time. I know he's hiding out somewhere close. I figure he must have contacted you to meet him somewhere. That's why you came here."

She desperately tried to figure out a plan to help herself. She suspected if she made up a story he would see through the lie in a moment. If she told him about her plan to meet her father at Artist's Palette, might she be putting her mother in danger along with her father?

Come alone...for Birdie.

The truth might get her killed, but she couldn't see any other way. After a deep breath, she said. "I won't tell you anything. Find him yourself."

He fired.

The shot was so loud she thought her eardrums would rupture. She screamed as the bullet plowed into the floorboards at her feet, inches from Chunk's arthritic legs. He yelped and whined, frantic with fear. She tried to snatch him up, but Max stopped her.

"Don't you dare," she panted.

His voice was low and earnest. "I won't hesitate again. I'll start with the dog, hurt him as many times as I have to until you'll tell me anything."

"Monster," she said, blinking to keep the tears from falling.

"It's business."

"Someone will hear the shots," she murmured.

"I don't think it will take that long. You love animals, always have. You won't be able to stand seeing this old geezer dying in pain."

Anger almost choked her. "What happened to make you such a soulless man?"

"Life, honey," he said, eyes glittering. "Life. Next shot kills the dog or maybe just hurts him real bad."

"No," she whispered, a hand around the whimpering animal at her ankle.

"I'm listening."

She swallowed hard. She had to save him, save them both. Suddenly, she jerked her head toward the front of the shop, pretending as if she'd heard something.

Max was immediately on the alert, twisting to see for himself. "What?"

"Nothing," she said, lips pressed tight. There was no need to fake any tension; that was clear in her voice. "I didn't hear anything."

But her ruse worked. Max took two steps away from her, peering toward the front window to check the street. Pilar didn't hesitate. In a flash she was running with Chunk and sprinting out the back door.

TEN

Austin drove the fire trail at an insane speed, the dogs fighting to keep their positions on the seat next to him.

"We'll find Ethel, don't worry," he told them. Maybe he'd been wrong about the ruse, he tried to tell himself. Pilar would be waiting patiently at the shop, talking things over with Jude. He used the hands-free mechanism in his truck to dial.

"Call Pilar," he said over the sound of rocks kicking up against the wheels.

The phone rang and rang until a mechanical voice mail picked up.

The person you are calling is not available.

He pressed the gas harder. Why hadn't he stopped to think before he'd raced off to find the dogs? Any idiot would have realized whoever cut the fence had done so for a reason. Max was the kind of guy who didn't do anything without a reason.

The headlights pierced the darkness as he drew closer to the shop. Jouncing back onto the paved road he stomped on the brakes as Pilar appeared through the gloom, her hair streaming out to become part of the night sky. Behind her, Max sprinted, his bulky form barreling through the night. Austin slammed the truck to stop and leaped out. Slipping on the gravel, he lunged at Max, who could not stop his forward momentum in time. Austin got him by the shirt as he tried to grab something from his pocket.

"He's got a gun," Pilar shouted.

Austin held Max's wrists as they tumbled into a heap. Strong as Austin was, he was hampered by his shoulder. Sweat poured off him and suddenly Pilar was there and so were the dogs.

"No, Pilar," he wanted to shout at her,

but she was reaching around Max, poking her fingers into his eyes.

Max grunted and shook her off, but the effort cost him leverage, and Austin used the advantage to try to pin him. He'd nearly managed, but Waffles had leaped into the fray, barking, hopping up and down on his back paws, unsure what to do. He tried to worm his way between Max and Austin. One moment, Austin thought he'd immobilized Max and the next, Waffles shoved his face into Austin's. The momentarily surprise was all Max needed. He broke free with a grunt and ran into the darkness.

Austin lay panting. Pilar appeared unharmed and the relief dizzied him. Waffles licked his cheeks. "You're a lover, not a fighter, aren't you, Waffles?"

He sat up. Pilar knelt next to him. She did not appear to be harmed. As if reading her mind, she said, "I tricked him into thinking the police had arrived. He…" She swallowed. "He was going to shoot

Chunk to make me tell him about the meet with Dad."

And then she was crying, and he was looping her into his arms, comforting, while Waffles went to tend to Lucy and Chunk, who sat together shivering. Guilt left a bitter taste in his mouth. She was unhurt because she'd taken care of herself, instead of him doing what he should have done to protect her.

"I'm sorry," he said. He stroked his hands over her hair, soft and silky as he remembered, the delicate curve of her ears, her neck. He remembered how she'd used to make that little sweet sigh when he'd snuggled her close.

Way back when...

Before she'd left him...

He felt just the first flush of bitterness, but this time it died away in place of something else. It floored him, sitting on that patch of rocky ground that there were mountains of ways he had not properly cared for nor appreciated the woman tucked into the crook of his arm. He'd been too wrapped up in himself, too prideful, and those qualities had grown to embarrassing proportions after his injury. He wanted to tell her what was in his mind then, to spool the words into the soft desert air and make sense of them.

But they didn't make sense.

She'd left him.

And that was unforgivable. Wasn't it?

He put a few inches between them while he caught his breath. His phone rang.

"I'm at the shop. Where are you?" Jude barked.

"On our way back. Max cornered Pilar there but she ran. He was heading north up the fire trail, but I suspect he corrected course to double back to the road. He won't take his chance in the ravine."

"I'm en route. Go…"

"I know," Austin said, before he clicked off. Go back to the shop where he should have stayed in the first place. He got to his feet and helped Pilar up. Her fingers were ice cold, but she was not shaking too much. They climbed into the truck, Chunk in her lap and Waffles and Lucy jammed between them.

"Where's Ethel?" Pilar said.

He swallowed. "I couldn't find her."

Her mouth fell open. "Oh, no. We have to go search."

"I will, as soon as we talk to Jude and get my brother to come keep watch at the shop."

"But I can help—" She broke off. "I'm sorry. That's a silly idea. Oh, Austin. I feel terrible about Ethel."

"My fault."

"No," she said. "Mine. I brought this all on you when I came back to Furnace Falls."

"No, you brought this all on me when you left." He tensed. What was he doing? Trying to remind himself he was better off without her? "I apologize. That was uncalled for."

She didn't answer, bending her head over Chunk.

He heaved out a breath. "Listen, I shouldn't have left you alone. I ran off, letting my emotions get the better of my good sense. I am beginning to realize that's a pattern for me."

She continued to cuddle the dog. They were almost to the shop when she finally responded, almost looking at him, but not quite. "You made the best decision you could at the moment. I wouldn't hold that against you."

And she wouldn't. Pilar was sincere. She'd forgiven him so many times for his impulsivity, excused his bad moods after the injury, his curtness, as if it was nothing. The notion was tantalizing, that forgiveness could be handed out so graciously, like letting go of a heavy weight by simply relaxing your grip.

There wasn't enough forgiveness in him then to expunge what she'd done. That would take an act of grace, and he didn't have nearly enough of that. Could he grow into that kind of person? He wasn't sure.

But he could treat her better, show her the man she deserved, even if they weren't meant to be a couple. He heaved in a breath. "Maybe God's teaching me patience the hard way."

She offered the barest whisper of a smile. "I never knew you to admit that you needed any."

"I need a whole lot of things." He touched her hand. "And it's beginning to dawn on me that you needed more from me than I gave you. I'm sorry for that too."

The glimmer in her eyes told him she was moved by his admission. "We both made mistakes." She leaned over and kissed his cheek, a friendly kiss, with a hint of an apology in it, but it echoed through him like a hammer on iron. "I want to get through this without causing you any more trouble."

Get through this…

And that's what he wanted too. Nothing more.

With Waffles and Lucy in tow, they drove back to the shop.

Pilar paced after Jude, Levi and Austin had left.

Jude had added fuel to the disappointment fire with his update. "Spent hours on the phone, but I found the cigar shop. No help there. Max stops in personally, pays in cash. No credit trail. I left pictures and the guy may or may not call me if Max comes in again. He absolutely denies illegally selling Cuban cigars in the first place, so his word is not exactly above reproach."

As she did another lap around the shop area, Chunk whined and snuffled. Waffles and Lucy would not settle either, worried at their missing companion. Levi had arrived with Seth, and immediately left again with Austin to hunt for the lost dog while Seth stayed with her. She tried not to notice the rifle he had propped inconspicuously in the corner. He sat in a chair and held Chunk, making small talk about the weather until she couldn't stand it anymore.

"The terrain's bad out there," she finally said. "Isn't it? Ethel's such a small dog and timid. She could have been..." She couldn't finish.

Seth leaned forward, forearms propped on his knees. "No point in considering the 'could haves.' That's one thing I've learned through all this physical therapy after I got shot. Work with what you have at the moment instead of what might have been. If Ethel is out there alive, Austin and Levi will find her. They've both got that uncanny wilderness gene." He sighed and rubbed his leg. "Even before I had the accident, I sure didn't. I lose my car in the parking lot on a regular basis." He grinned. "Still trying to shed my city slicker image. Don't worry, though. I know how to shoot if it comes to that."

She knew from Austin that Seth had been in a coma after having survived a shooting. It was a relief, in a way, to talk to someone who hadn't been in town for her untimely departure. She thought about what had happened not an hour ago with Max, and her legs went wobbly.

Seth's green eyes were warm. "Can I get you some water? Tea?"

"No, thank you. I was remembering... uh..." She swallowed. "I'm going to go upstairs for a bit, okay?"

Seth nodded. "Sure thing. I'll keep the fort secure. Chunk will help me."

But when she headed for the stairs, Chunk began to whine for her. Waffles and Lucy circled noses, but Chunk would not be comforted. He deserved some spoiling after his fright. He certainly didn't want to go back out into the scary backyard or be left with a man he didn't know. She scooped him up and lugged him along with her.

Settling him on the bed upstairs, she realized with a start that it was past seven. She yanked her phone from her pocket. One missed call. No message. She sent a quick text.

Mom, I'm sorry I missed your call. Please call now.

The minutes ticked slowly. She gripped the phone. The hour came and went. Five torturous minutes, ten, fifteen. Fear overtook her and she dialed the number from which her mother's text had come.

It rang repeatedly. "Mom, where are you? I need to talk to you," she murmured, but there was no answer to that. Shivering with the cumulative shock of the evening, she sank down on the bed to pray that God would take care of her mother, wherever she was.

A clamor from the shop an hour later

caused her to hurry downstairs. One look at Austin told her they had not found Ethel. She told them about the missed call from her mother's phone.

Levi exchanged a telling look with Austin.

"What?" she said.

"The call was probably not from your mother," Austin said. "More likely it was from Max, making sure you'd be here waiting for that call so he could corner you after he let the dogs out."

She let that sink in, recalling the strange nonanswer Max had given when she asked him if he knew her mother's whereabouts. "Or he could have known we were helping at the hotel. Figured we'd be home after the dinner hour. Do you think he has her?" Their carefully guarded expressions led to another horrifying thought. "Or he's killed her?"

Austin took her hand and squeezed. "There would be no profit in that for him, would there? If he had her, he'd tell you so to pressure you into giving up your father."

"But if he doesn't have her, why isn't she calling me?"

The gentle pressure of his fingers increased. "We'll find out." They bid goodnight to Levi and Seth.

He fixed them bowls of canned soup, which neither of them had much of an appetite for, after they fed the dogs.

"They'll be sleeping inside tonight and every night." The slight hitch in his voice gave him away. He was worrying about the poor missing dog. "Until I get a better handle on things."

Until Max was caught...until Ethel was found...but those things might never happen. She shivered, and he stroked a finger along her forearm.

"It has been traumatic tonight. Are you...okay?"

She forced a cheerful nod. "Yes." She shuddered. "Max is terrible. Worse than I thought. I keep remembering him standing there with that gun. He would have killed Chunk, no question in my mind."

His eyes glimmered. "If you don't want to stay here, I can find another place. A couple of rented rooms in Beattie that will take dogs. We can hole up there if you'd feel better."

How tender he was, trying to comfort her when she knew his heart was torn in two with worry about Ethel. Her mind traveled back into the past. She remembered the moment, the precise moment, she got the phone call from Max.

If you don't give me what I want, I will kill your blond boyfriend. I'm patient, and I can stick around forever.

And in that moment, she'd considered telling Austin everything, trusting that he would be able to stay safe, with a hefty dose of caution. That he would not charge off in search of Max. But Austin was not a "play it safe" kind of man, and she knew that in time he'd resent any restrictions on his freedom. He'd chafed against the physical limitations imposed by his accident, certainly. It was unfair to ask of him.

Yet it had been unfair not to, to leave instead in such a way.

The shop light gleamed on his hair, accentuating the lines around his mouth, which she had not noticed before. He was more careworn and scuffed around the edges than she'd remembered. Even his smile was more sedate, less wild than it had been. Her heart thunked when she realized that she found him more attractive than before.

You'd better keep that nonsense to yourself. A future with Austin was a tissue paper dream, fragile, tenuous, destroyed with one simple dose of logic. *You left him. He'll never forgive you.*

Still, she wished her pulse did not speed up when he cast that blue-green gaze her way.

She blinked herself out of her thoughts. "That is very thoughtful to arrange another place, but I am okay. Unless, you'd rather I didn't stay here."

"I want you here." He looked startled by his own words and quickly removed his hand from her arm. "I mean, the shop's the best place. Levi's gone to the hardware store. It's closed now, but he'll get the owner to open it up. He's buying a new lock for the back door. I should have replaced it ages ago. Never know when you'll get some teen looking to vandalize." He was up and prowling around, picking up the soup bowls, throwing away paper napkins. Nervous, she thought with a start. Nervous? She did not recall ever seeing the self-assured Austin nervous. Why would he be? Because he'd said he wanted her to stay?

No. Must be nothing more than the agitation of having Ethel missing.

"I'll repay you for the expenses," she said.

"Not necessary. What do you do for a

living, by the way? Writing that botany book?"

Austin had always encouraged her to write the book, ever since she'd mentioned it to him. Sometimes it felt as if he believed in the project more than she believed she could actually accomplish it. *The world needs a desert botany book about all the wild and wacky plants that grow here. Most people have no idea about the delicacy of the environment.* He'd grinned to be using the exact phrase she'd parroted so many times. *You're just the person to write it. If you can teach a dope like me to name an endangered wildflower, you can do anything.*

Funny how she'd forgotten about that. "I'm working on it when I have time, but I make my living as a web designer."

He arched an eyebrow. "Really? Didn't think you'd go for a tech job. You were always more into nature than cyber stuff."

"I had to find a job that I could do from home," she said quietly.

"Because you were worried about Uncle Max?"

She nodded. "I didn't know I had to be until... Well, after the car accident I stopped working on my master's and got the tech job. I used to work on the website for the college botany department, so it was an easy transition."

His mouth tightened. "Pilar, Max messed up your life in the past, but we're going to make sure he doesn't get to control your choices in the future."

Hope sparked in her heart. If only she could be free of Max...how would her life look different? The tint of Austin's eyes was the perfect blend of spring and autumn. She could almost lose herself in that glow. Startled, she looked away. *Tissue paper dreams...remember?* "There is something I can do to help with Ethel," she said. She found her laptop and tapped open the screen. "We can post a lost dog flyer on all the local sites, including the Sunshine site."

"That would be great," he said. "I was going to call them in the morning, but it would help to have a picture of Ethel. He sent a photo to her phone. "This is a good one. She was wearing this silly striped sweater that Willow gave her. I didn't want to put it on." He gave her a pained look. "I mean, there are frills and a bow and everything, but Ethel was cold in the evenings." He stared at the photo with undisguised sadness.

Impulsively, she hugged him. He went still for a moment, and then his arms wrapped around her waist, pulling her close, head bent. "We'll find her," she whispered. And she rubbed his back, like she used to do when they dreamed of a future together, when life was a straightforward trip instead of a snarl of twisting roads and dead-end alleys. He kissed her cheek, his lips leaving a circle of warmth before he restored the distance between them.

"Thanks. I... I don't want to think about

her being lost out there in the dark. She'll be scared. She's timid anyway."

"I'll post it on the web right now. People can be crummy, sometimes, but if you post a picture of a lost dog, they come out of the woodwork to help."

He cocked his head. "Really?"

"Really." It made her feel happy to think that in some small way she might be able to soothe Austin's heartache. What a strange reversal of fortune.

Not fortune, she thought. God was allowing her to help the man she'd so grievously hurt. *Thank you, Lord*, she thought as she tapped the keys, the tiniest bit of warmth lingering from the spot where he'd kissed her.

ELEVEN

The days passed in an agony of slow motion. By the time the weekend rolled to a close, Austin was an efficient dinner server at the Hostprings, but his frustration that Max hadn't been found was almost intolerable. The distraction was welcome, since there was also no sign of Ethel for all his efforts, and Pilar's mother had not called either. Jude posted a unit on the long sweeping hotel drive, so there was no way Max could slip by without notice. They were treading waters that seemed to rise every moment, the time ticking down until the meeting with Pilar's father at Artist's Palette.

Jude had already put plans in place to capture Cyrus. He'd also agreed to look into the mysterious cell phone situation with Pilar's mom. Jude was not sharing any particulars with them of his official arrangements or inquiries. Cop protocols aside, Austin knew that Jude still didn't trust Pilar. Like a bolt out of the blue, Austin had to acknowledge that he did. He believed everything she'd told him, and what's more he knew she wasn't going to bail out until she'd done all she could for her mother and father, the people who had turned her life upside down.

Trust Pilar? The thought struck him with such unexpected force that he dropped a bowl of chicken tortilla soup on the kitchen floor during the Sunday dinner service. Well, it wasn't so shocking was it? Pilar had never lied to him. And it wasn't like he was fixing to restart their relationship, anyway. No, the sapphire engagement ring was still safe in his pencil drawer where he'd tossed it, and there would never be any chance Pilar would be his bride. So he advised himself to forget kissing her as he mopped up the spilled soup.

But he still felt the softness of her cheek, the tender embrace that was so familiar but so different. He could not explain to himself why his brain took leave of his body where Pilar was concerned.

As he washed what he thought was the last dish, Pilar came into the kitchen with another stack. He huffed out a breath and flicked a bit of foam in her direction. "No more. I've got dishpan hands," he said pitifully. "You're killing me."

"We'll buy you some rubber gloves," was his sister Willow's unsympathetic reply from her place at the stove waiting for Herm's next filled platter.

Willow's animosity toward Pilar was thawing a fraction, he thought, as they worked hard side by side. Maybe she was beginning to trust Pilar, as well. He couldn't think why that pleased him. All right, so he trusted her with everything but his heart. That he was keeping to himself.

When the service was done, Willow wiped down the kitchen counter while he and Pilar loaded leftovers into the fridge. "Laney said to tell everyone the back room needs to be cleaned after the painting if we have any extra time," Willow said. "That's where the wedding reception will be. Seth's bringing over some wedding favors Mara made, but he has to help Levi with a wildflower excursion today." She looked at the wall clock. "I'm sorry, guys. I have a tour also. Spring is hopping, so to speak. Is there any way…?"

"Yes," Pilar said immediately. "I'll do it."

Though Austin had wanted to take another drive of the area in search of Ethel, he wasn't about to leave Pilar alone, even at the Hotsprings. Plus there was no way he would disappoint Laney. The more she could rest and not worry about the hotel, the better for both her and the baby.

"I'm in too," he said. "Let's go see what we're up against."

The room was a long rectangular space with a tiled floor and massive windows positioned to show off the view of the Inyo Mountains. Though there were tarps draped over the floor, the walls sported the same drab brown paint they had for decades, not the lighter tint Laney had chosen. "Painter hasn't gotten to this room yet. We'll have to clean it another night," Austin said. "Hope Laney doesn't find out. At least we can fold up the tables to make it quicker for Gary when he gets here."

He took hold of one end of the table and she the other, and they flipped it on its side to collapse the legs. A lance of white-hot pain made him cry out and clutch his shoulder. She hurried to him.

"Are you…?" She stopped, hands outstretched as though she wanted to touch him. Then she stood silently, lip caught between her teeth.

Before, he knew what he would have said.

I'm fine.

Just a twinge.

Don't treat me like I'm damaged.

I'll be the exact same as I was before, no matter what the doctors or God or anyone else says about it.

This time, a thought stripped the retorts away. Humility would bring him grace.

He cleared his throat. "I should probably ice it. That helps when I have a flare-up. Might have aggravated it in the scuffle with Max." In fact, the tendons had been screaming at him, disrupting his sleep, but he wouldn't confess to that.

She scooted off and returned with a bag of ice wrapped in a kitchen towel. They sat on folding chairs while he applied it. He inhaled the deepest breath he could manage. "The doctors and therapists have done what they can. I'm…probably not going to regain full motion," he said in a rush. "Ever." It was the first time he'd said that aloud.

Her response was soft, but carefully neutral. "I'm sorry to hear that."

He read her expression. "I was depressed for a long time, probably still am a little, to be honest."

"Understandable." Still the careful tone.

"I'll keep up with the exercises, but I've had to admit to myself that I'm not going to be the same person I was before." He watched for her reaction.

She stared and a kind of wonder crept over her. "I've come to the same conclusion about myself."

He raised an eyebrow. No, after what she'd been through, she wouldn't ever be the same. How come she wasn't bitter, angry, hateful about it?

As if she'd read his mind, she answered. "But you know what? We weren't meant to stay the same, and I'm glad I'm not the person I was."

He locked eyes with her. "I understand what you mean, but I can't say I'm happy I won't be able to climb anymore."

"I get it. I'm not rejoicing that my family life is a mess and I don't look like myself anymore either." She looked down and he found himself nudging her chin up.

"You're beautiful, Pilar. You always were and you always will be."

She colored a deep shade of crimson, and he leaned back. What was he doing? But the words slipped out clean and easy like new roots cleaving the ground. "I'm beginning to think God's growing me up against my will," he said ruefully. "You too?"

Her smile was brilliant. "Me too."

"But I sure wish He could give me some lessons that didn't hurt so much."

She laughed and he joined in. Things were easy and light between them, if only for a few days, a break from the terror and uncertainty that enveloped them.

"I, uh… I think I probably can't help you move that table," he said sadly. "I'm afraid I might drop my end."

Still, she sported that wondrous smile. "No problem. This place is piled high with helpers." She called to Willow who came in frowning.

"I was on my way out. What's wrong?" she demanded of her brother. "Do you need a doctor?"

He held up a hand. "No, just trying to accept my limitations without making things worse."

Willow's eyes rounded. "What? Can that actually be a ray of common sense coming out of my brother's excessively thick skull? Now I've seen everything." She turned a calculating look on Pilar. "Is this your doing? How'd you manage it?"

"Willow," he said, forestalling any embarrassing conversation, "how about helping Pilar move the table?"

Willow assisted with the maneuver, a

pleased smile lingering on her lips as she said goodbye to Pilar.

As they drove back to the shop, Austin tracked the progress of three vultures in the sky, circling a prospective meal. What if…

Pilar touched his wrist. "I know Ethel's going to be all right."

How had she known he was worrying about that? Because she'd always known. It felt strange and freeing to realize he didn't have to hide behind a glib remark to show he was in control. Instead, he reached for her hand and squeezed it in his own.

"Maybe tomorrow," he said.

Tomorrow.

The word sent a chill through his cloud of warmth. Tomorrow they'd meet her father at Artist's Palette. Would Pilar get the answers she needed? Or was Cyrus using her for his dangerous dirty work? Tomorrow might change both their lives forever.

* * *

When she arrived downstairs on Monday morning, dressed and ready, Austin already had the new locks on the back door. His tools were put away, the paint retouched in typical fastidious fashion. Clearly he had not slept much. Waffles, Lucy and Chunk lay in a pile together on the bark-o-lounger. Was it her imagination, or were they acting dejected, pining for their lost family member? She did the mental math... Ethel had been missing now for more than three days. Was she hurt? Scared? Cold or hungry? Or worse?

"I took the dogs out for a good long romp in the yard, but they spent most of the time searching for Ethel," he said.

She wished she had a way to cheer him up. "I checked for messages." Pilar sighed, with an ache in her heart. "No response to our missing dog post yet."

Austin did not look at her. "I was afraid of that. Levi went out again with Seth last night." And Austin hadn't been able to join them because he was saddled with protecting her, she thought grimly.

"They've started searching from the other side of the ravine in case she managed to get that far, but nothing that I've heard." He paused. "Are you ready for this meet today?"

He had as much reason as she did to want the matter over with. Certainly, her presence had done nothing but complicate his life, in spite of the flickers of warmth she felt between them. The knot of tension in her stomach belied her reply. "Yes. It's time to get this over with. But I'd be lying if I said I wasn't scared. I don't even know my father, not really. I'm thinking lately maybe I never did."

There were flashes of fond memories, the father-daughter fishing trip where they didn't catch anything but a discarded sock. The construction of an elaborate bird feeder out of Popsicle sticks. Mostly, he was gone a lot. "On the road" her mother would say. They must have been struggling financially, with her mother working at the convenience store and her father an appliance repairman. Yes, they'd moved a lot, but she'd not realized it was probably due to rent increases they couldn't afford. Austin brought her out of her reverie.

"Everything is going to turn out fine. Jude has made arrangements, and so have I."

"What kind of arrangements?"

He shrugged. "Backup."

She did not want Austin to risk anything else for her. The growing feelings she felt for him were bad enough. She could not endure it if he lost anything further, besides his beloved dog. What she'd already done to him was guilt enough for a lifetime. She was about to launch into another pitch for her to meet her father alone, but he grabbed his pack and held the door for her. Unable to think of any other way to discourage him, she went outside and climbed in the truck.

After they entered Death Valley National Park, it was only a thirty-minute journey to Artist's Palette. The drive along Badwater Road was festooned with the colors of spring wildflowers. It was not a super bloom, since that rare phenomenon occurred only after an unusually wet winter, but there was a respectable showing from the temporary blossoms. They would continue to open their faces to welcome the desert sunshine as the day progressed. How she wished she could relax and do the same. Instead, her stomach was cramped with tension. Would she really meet her father? This man who was supposed to care for her?

The buildings of Furnace Creek greeted them, the "hub" of the national park itself. The "town" boasted a visitor's center, two hotels and numerous campgrounds, as well as a few places to eat, a post office and gas station. There were many visitors strolling through the area, prime tourist season since the highs would only reach the low nineties this early in the spring. Austin turned on to Artist's Drive. The plentitude of dips and curves would normally have thrilled her, but at the moment, she was struggling to keep her heaving stomach in check. There were dozens of other cars on the road. Typical, since Artist's Palette was a "must see" for tourists.

The gorgeous spot was always bustling during the cooler months. With so many camera-toting visitors, how would she ever find her father? There were lots of small hiking trails in and around the main viewing area. So many places where her father might be waiting, watching. Austin peered into each and every vehicle as they found a parking place.

"I don't see a police car," she said. "Where's Jude?"

"Not sure, but he's probably close. Civilian car, maybe."

"And your backup?"

Austin smiled. "Don't worry. If you have a Duke for backup, they'll be there when you need them. Levi's in place. Ready?"

Breath gone shallow, she nodded. They got out, mingling with the visitors checking out the multihued vistas. Every person who came close earned a hard stare from Austin, who was glued to her elbow. All the visitors she spotted were absorbed in the magnificent view or pointing to the various hiking trails that splayed out from the area like meandering rivers of sand.

"I don't see him," she whispered. What if he didn't show? She'd been so worried about the alternative. Sunlight beat down on her, ramping up her tension.

The light coaxed the pink and green from the twisted rocks, earning admiration from the tourists. Suddenly she found it painful to look at. There was no one matching her father's description anywhere. Turning slowly, she continued to search.

Dad, where are you?

One of the tourists with binoculars around his neck, wrinkled his sunburned nose as he approached. Austin stepped in front of her.

Her nerves ratcheted tight, until she realized this was not her father.

"Excuse me," the man asked. "Do you have a map? My…" He broke off, mouth gone slack with shock. What had upset him? Struggling to decipher his expression, she saw he was staring over her shoulder. A second later the sound of a revving engine cut through the air.

In a blur, a speeding motorcycle hurtled toward them. The churning wheels lifted a cloud of choking sand and dust. Austin shoved her out of the way, pitching forward onto his stomach in the process. Jude appeared from the crowd, wearing civilian clothes and hollering into his radio before he leaped into an unmarked car, pursuing the departing motorcycle. Pilar got to her feet, wiping grit from her face. Confused and panicked visitors scattered in every direction, obscuring Austin from her view.

"Austin?" she called. Something had gone wrong, very wrong.

Amid the chaos and swirling dust, her father appeared. As she opened her mouth to scream, he lifted her off her feet and dragged her down the nearest trail. She tried to fight and pull away, but it was all she could do to maintain her footing on the steep slope. Where was he taking her? She kicked and connected with his shin, but he did not slow.

He pulled her behind one boulder, then another, while she struggled to free herself from his strong grasp. Coughing at the dust trapped in her nose and mouth, eyes streaming, she did not recognize the twisting trail along which she was being hauled. When she finally stopped coughing and dug in her feet, he could not move her anymore. Yanking free, she turned to find herself backed up against a sun-warmed boulder, concealed from view by a shelf of rough-textured rock. They might as well be miles away, for the terrible isolation she felt. This man before her might be her father, but she felt only fear.

The dust slowly settled. Chest heaving, she rubbed her wrist, staring into a face she'd only seen for a moment for the last decade and a half. "Austin," she screamed, "I'm down here."

She opened her mouth to scream again when he surged forward and flattened his hand across her lips. She ripped the fingers away and was about to shriek with everything in her when he said the one thing that would stop her.

"Your mom is going to die if you don't help me."

"What?" she gasped.

His chapped lips twitched, rough and peeling. "I need you to listen, Peanut. I don't have much time."

Don't call me Peanut, she wanted to holler. Instead, she inhaled, fighting for calm.

His eyes were heavily pouched, his clothes even more disheveled than when she'd seen him at the campsite. He was sunburned, thin, his collarbones clearly visible at the gap in his torn shirt. There was a glimmer there, of the father she remembered, something in the cheeks and the way his head was weighted forward on his neck, like a thoughtful bird's.

"You look a little different from the pictures your mom sent me in prison, but I recognized your profile anyway." His mouth went tight. "The accident, right? Mom told me about that too. I am sorry. I didn't realize my choices would result in you being hurt. If I had... I never would have agreed to Max's plan." She heard his breathing go shallow, a pleading note creeping in. "I thought it would be an easy way to get us in the black. A couple of hours and no one would get hurt." He raised a hand to touch her cheek, but she jerked back.

"You dragged me down here against my will. What kind of a father does that? Your choices changed my whole life. Everything, Dad, everything." Fury slammed through her.

"I know. I'll make it up to you, some-day. I promise."

"Save your promises. I'm not interested in your apologies. You arranged an elab-orate scheme to get me to Furnace Falls, dragged Austin and an old helpless dog into it. All right. It worked. Here I am. All yours. Tell me why I'm here and what it's got to do with Mom."

He scrubbed a gnarled hand through his shaggy gray hair. "I made so many mis-takes and I can't fix any of them." She noticed his fingers were shaking.

"Yes, you can. Give the police the money or tell them where it is, if you know. Max won't get his mitts on it, and he won't have any more reason to stalk me or Mom."

"I can't do that."

"Because you don't want to go back to jail?"

Slowly he shook his head. "No, Peanut. I admit, I hid the money. I was going to retrieve it when I got out of jail, but now it's the only bargaining chip I have to keep your mother alive."

She recoiled, her head whacking into the rocks. "What do you mean? What's going on?"

He listened for a moment. "They'll find me soon."

She resisted the urge to grab him by the shirtfront. "Then tell me now. Quick."

"Your mom. She's in trouble. That's why I tricked you into coming here. I wasn't sure there was any other secure way, and I needed to get you away from the apartment. Your mother said he was watching the house, possibly bugged your phone."

"What's happened to Mom?" Pilar said through grated teeth.

"He has her."

Pilar's body went cold. "Max?"

He nodded. "Imprisoned somewhere. He figures he'll trade her for the money, but she must not be cooperating, which is why he's coming after you. Or..."

Or she's already dead.

"Oh, Dad," she whispered. "She called last night, but I missed it. I sent her a text question to be sure if was really her, but he must be forcing her to answer." Was she really hearing this? Could it be that her mom was imprisoned? Nausea swept through her in a sickening wave.

"Any other calls?"

She shook her head.

"My phone was stolen," he said, eyes drifting in thought, "but I know she would not have left you if she'd had a choice, not now. She told me Max was stalking you." He sucked in an unsteady breath. "I told her I'd take care of it."

"But Mom doesn't know you hid the money, does she?" She had to force out the question. Her mother had lied about her father. Had she lied about the stolen money too?

He shook his head. "I was going to take it and get settled, tell her I'd gotten a good job, send for you both. Birdie wouldn't have come if she knew it was the stolen money."

The breath whooshed out of her. "But Max will never let you have it," Pilar said with a feeling of defeat. "He'll kill all of us to get his hands on that money." A shudder shook through her. And now it looked like he'd start with her mother.

TWELVE

Austin struggled to his feet, finding himself amidst a bunch of alarmed tourists. They were all standing around, postures tense, poised to flee, but the motorcyclist had not returned to do any more mischief. Had it been Pilar's father? He didn't think so.

Frantically, he looked in every direction. His shout froze on his lips when his cell pinged. Levi.

He took her down into the trails. Meet me at ours.

Austin knew exactly which one "ours" was. He and Levi used to hike every trail they could find as young teens, the more difficult, the better. He'd always enjoyed having Levi to himself, without Willow around, though he'd never tell her. Their "twinness" was often a bridge he could not cross, unless she was off doing something with her friends. The best hiking season was the earliest blush of summer when the temperatures were beginning to be inhospitable to visitors but had not reached their peak of ferocity. Then they'd had the desert to themselves...or at least it had felt like it.

Their favorite trail in this vicinity started with a gentle slope that surged immediately into a heart thumpingly steep ascent. From the apex, they'd be able to see everything. He would quickly find Pilar, he had to. Who knew what her father meant to do? He struggled to keep his nerves in check as he called Jude with the information.

Jude sounded out of breath when he answered.

"I got him. Looks like Cyrus made a

deal with this kid. Twenty bucks in exchange for a diversion. Doesn't seem like the connection is any deeper than that." He paused. "I'll be there as soon as I can. Be careful, we don't know what Cyrus is capable of."

Oh, they had some idea all right...robbery, injury to Pete Silvers, dragging his daughter into the middle of it all. Austin clicked off and jogged down the slope before he began to take the ascent as fast as he could. The steep pitch was certainly more of a challenge after he'd been away from rock climbing for six months. It aggravated him to find himself puffing, his muscles hollering at him as he caught up with Levi. Let them holler, he figured, teeth gritted against the pain. He was going to get Pilar away from her criminal father no matter how much his body screamed at him.

He passed two hikers with heavy backpacks.

"What's the hurry?" one of them asked as he elbowed by.

Ignoring them, he made it to the top a moment after his brother. Levi didn't stop to talk.

"There." He pointed, and they took off for a dusty trail.

"From here we can get the drop on him," Levi said, hurrying through a narrow rock fissure. Austin noticed he was not breathing hard at all. He delved deeper into the grit he'd used before in his days of scaling cliffs. "Did he hurt her? Could you tell?"

"Saw him drag her in a crevice. Remember that one that forms sort of a cave? With the rocks that look like teeth?"

He did. They hiked as fast as they could along the uneven trail. In spite of his long legs, he could not overtake Levi. "Hey," he said, finally pulling even. "I feel duty bound to tell you that Mara wouldn't want you putting yourself at risk. We know it wasn't Cyrus who fired the flare gun, but we don't know much else about him."

Levi didn't slow one iota. "If he knows anything about how to find the guy who fired on my horses, he's gonna tell me."

The determined clench of Levi's jaw made it clear that nothing had been forgotten where Levi's horses were concerned. They stopped short at the entrance to the barest scratch of a trail that would lead them to the cave.

"All right," Levi whispered. "Couple feet in and we'll be able to see."

"And they'll see us. Any way out the back?"

"Only a sharp drop-off into a wash."

"All right," Austin said. "Ready when you are."

He ticked off a silent count to three.

Pilar struggled to keep her thoughts from spinning off into panic. *Keep calm*, she told herself. *Find out what is going on.* "Dad, how do you know Max has Mom?"

"I got one frantic phone call from her a week ago."

The same time she'd disappeared from the apartment.

"She said, 'Please give him what he wants or...'"

Pilar swallowed. "Or what?"

His skin paled under the sunburn. "'Or he'll kill me.'"

A faint buzzing sounded in her ears. She heard a shout, someone getting closer to their hiding place.

Her father heard it too. He swiveled his head, searching for an escape route.

"We have to tell the police," she pressed.

"They can't fix this. You don't know Max like I do. He's ruthless and he doesn't care who he hurts."

"I know him better than you think," she snapped. She wondered if Max had sent the text message, pretending to be her mother, as some sort of a ruse. But the caller had known there was no Cousin Ellen, so might it really have been from her mother? She'd escaped Max somehow? A thought chilled her. Or had she been persuaded to hand over that information by force?

He's ruthless, and he doesn't care who he hurts. She remembered him threatening to shoot Chunk. There was no doubt in her mind that he would have done it, if the situation had played out differently.

Her father looked around and then focused on her, lines of worry grooved around his mouth. "Pilar, I know how we can save her. You need to get the money I hid. If I try, he'll spot me for sure. If I get the cops involved, they'll take the money and I'll have no way to save her."

"This is ridiculous. I'm not going to help you retrieve stolen money."

He wasn't listening, his eyes were roving the piles of silvered rock, looking for pursuers. "You have to go and get it. It's the only way. Bring it to me."

"So you can run away with it?" She almost laughed aloud. "Why should I trust you? Why should Mom?"

He winced. "I deserve what you think

of me. I am a bad father, but I love your mother and she knows it. Birdie always did her best by me when I gave her so little in return. I have to get her away from him. The money is my only bargaining chip."

"But it's not your money to use, Dad. Can't you see that?"

He snatched up her hand and squeezed, his damp palm pressing hard. She felt the desperation through that contact. "It's the only way to save her. I know it's not right, but I have nothing else."

Her pulse had ratcheted to a fever pitch, but she detached her hand as calmly as she could. "Where is the money?"

He paused. "In a storage unit in Las Vegas. We rented it years ago, when we were first married, and your mom's been keeping up the payments. She doesn't know that's where I hid it in the three days before I was arrested. The cops never found out about the unit. I hid the money in an old ten-speed bike."

Pilar felt the blood drain from her face. She could hardly get a breath past the sudden wall of anxiety pressing down on her.

"What?"

"After I got out of the hospital, we moved to an apartment in Cliffton," she said slowly. "That's where you sent Austin to deliver your message."

"Austin, your fiancé. I was hoping it would work out like that. Your mom told me about him, and I found him on the dog website."

"My ex-fiancé."

He looked down for a moment until his eyes searched her face for more.

She swallowed. "I had to stay in the hospital for a couple of weeks after my surgery. During that time, Mom made new living arrangements for us. When I was released, we moved in. I asked her where she got the furnishings and rugs and such. She…she said she closed out a storage unit you used to rent."

"No, no," he whispered, shaking his head. "She couldn't have done that. She wouldn't have without asking me."

Pilar's anger flamed. "For years she had to take care of a child, find shelter and food by herself. She did what she had to, and she didn't have to ask permission of her incarcerated husband."

He grimaced. "I can't believe this."

"She didn't know, like you said," Pilar snapped. "She sent it all to a flea market."

His whole body sagged. "No."

"You don't have the right to blame her. She worked at the grocery store and with our two jobs we barely made the rent. Why pay for a storage unit full of things we didn't need?"

His eyes danced in panic. "She must have kept the bike. It was my old college bike. Maybe it's in the garage at your place in Cliffton."

"We don't have a garage at the apartment."

He groaned. "This can't be happening. Birdie—" He broke off.

"What are we going to do?"

He was frozen for a moment, and then he jerked as if an electric spark had touched him. "We have to stick together." He grabbed her wrist and started to pull her farther into the foothills. "I have a motorbike hidden nearby. I'll ride us somewhere we can hide while we figure out what to do."

"No," she said, yanking herself out of his grip. "I'm not going anywhere with you."

"You have to," he said. "Max doesn't know about the storage unit, so she might still be alive."

"Hold it right there," a voice shouted. Levi appeared from behind a boulder on one end of the trail, Austin behind him. Her father reacted quickly, leaping by her so fast she fell to one knee. Levi ran by her in a flash, as Austin skidded to a stop at her side. He helped her up and pulled her into an embrace. Her cheek pressed to his chest, she could feel the frantic thumping of his heart.

"Did he hurt you?" he said in her ear.

"No," she said. All at once she wanted nothing more than to stay in his arms, and pretend she didn't know the terrible situation her father had plunged them into. Austin's embrace was tangible comfort, and she gave herself permission to pretend for a minute that he still loved her, and she him. They were a pair, enjoying the absolute wonder of this sacred desert. There were no life or death decisions to be made, no painful past between them. Did he feel it too? The urge to forget everything else and grab hold of what they'd lost?

She didn't realize she was crying until he pulled her to arm's length, his roving gaze worried.

"What happened?"

There was so much she needed to say, such frightening details about her mother that everything fought to come out of her mouth and nothing did.

"It's okay," he said quietly, squeezing her forearms. "We'll go back to the truck. You can take your time and tell us when you can. All right?"

She nodded miserably. Levi appeared covered with dust. "He actually jumped over and went into the wash. Can you believe that? I took a tumble, and by the time I got myself upright he was gone."

"He won't get far," Austin said. "Jude will get the National Park Service to search."

"We shouldn't stay out here in the open. I'll take Pilar back to the shop and wait for Jude there. Thanks, Levi," he said, clasping his brother in a quick hug. He heard Levi's frustration in his aggravated exhale.

"Wish we'd gotten him."

Austin stayed quiet as he drove Pilar back after they thanked Levi. She felt numb and uncertain.

"Dad said Max has my mother, and he needs the money he hid to ransom her."

Her sudden remark startled Austin. He was clearly waiting for her to tell him more.

"The problem is my mother got rid of the old bike from the storage unit where he'd stashed it. She didn't know."

"Are you sure she didn't find the money?"

Pilar stiffened. "I... I think so. My mother lied about my dad being dead to protect me. She wouldn't have taken stolen money."

He touched her hand. "Right. I'm sorry I suggested it."

But she could see why he had, with her train wreck of a family situation. "Dad doesn't want me to go to the police. I don't know what to do." She would have cried if she hadn't felt so utterly petrified.

Then he pressed her knuckle to his mouth and kissed it. It was such a fluid motion, so natural, but it echoed with the love they used to have. Twin pangs of sweet and bitter flowed through her. "I understand." He squeezed. "But Jude is a good man and a good cop. We have to share with him. Your dad has committed a crime, but maybe Jude can be flexible. I'll help you however I can, in whatever way I can, but the choice of how you want to proceed is up to you."

The choice was hers. And if she made the wrong one, her mother could die.

Swallowing hard, she closed her eyes and prayed.

Was it her imagination, or was Austin praying along with her?

Austin tried not to put any more demands on Pilar. He could tell she was deeply shaken by what she'd learned from her father. Everything in him screamed for action. They could do their own search, tear off into Death Valley Park and comb every corner in his truck or on horseback...but that was not safe or wise, and this was not his choice about how to handle things, it was hers. All he could do was join in with his feeble prayer.

This was not a situation he could control, or fix, or ignore. Humility was a hard lesson, but for some reason he knew he was a better man for trying to learn it. Beckett would be pleased, and that put a temporary smile on his face.

He sat as still as he could while she went upstairs and showered. When she came down, she looked calmer.

"I've been thinking hard and…"

He held his breath.

"As much as I'm worried about what my father will do next, I think the smartest thing is to ask Jude if he would start to search for my mother. He didn't want to before, but now there's good reason to believe she's in danger." She cast him an uncertain look. "Do you…does that seem like the right decision to you?"

He let out a breath and smiled. "I think that's exactly the right decision."

She pursed her lips. "You didn't even interrupt or suggest another option. Why not? Oh. Your list, right?"

"You'll be surprised to know, waiting patiently is not even in the top five, yet here I am giving it a go. I should totally get extra credit."

She laughed, and it eased the shadows from her face for a moment. "Yes, you should."

When Jude arrived, she told him everything that had passed between her and her father in the calmest manner she could muster.

He listened, asking only occasional clarifying questions. "I've already started that search in motion for your mother. With your permission, I'll have an officer friend of mine in Cliffton search your apartment to double-check she didn't accidentally bring that bike home and park it in a shed or something. They'll be discreet, in case Max is somehow keeping tabs on the place." He hooked his fingers on his gun belt, as if turning something over in his mind. "You've been through a lot, with your dad and such." He cleared his throat. "I would like to apologize for the way I treated you in my office when you first hit town."

She blinked in surprise. "I understand. I...hurt your cousin. Everyone has a reason to be angry with me."

"You had reasons too. Anyway—" he leaned forward "—we have a possible way to narrow down the search for your mother."

She gaped. "What? How?"

He looked slightly chagrined. "I know I said your mother's disappearance wasn't my business, but I had some people look into the cell phone tower transmissions anyway. The call you missed from your mom's phone was routed through a cell tower in an area about an hour east of here, an unincorporated area of Nevada. Wide-open land, rugged. Lots of area to search and we haven't found anything yet." He paused. "To be honest, I don't really have the resources to commit to much in the way of air support..."

"But I can," Austin said.

Jude grinned. "I was hoping you'd say that, cousin."

Austin was on his feet. "I'll file a flight plan now. I can be wheels-up in an hour."

"And you'll alert me instead of charging in anywhere, correct? I realize this is a stretch for you, Austin, since you usually act first and ask permission later. Pilar, I am counting on you to be the voice of reason."

She nodded, but she had her doubts about her own reasoning abilities just then.

Jude held up palm. "I'd like to remind you, though the text was sent from her number, there is absolutely no guarantee that your mother sent that message or that you're going to find anything at all in that wilderness."

Pilar heard with her ears, but not with

her heart. Now it was her turn to internalize the irrepressible optimism and energy that Austin conveyed in the taut lines of his body and the snap of purpose in his movements. They would find her mother before it was too late. They had to.

"Do you want to fly with me?" Austin asked her with a teasing smile.

"I sure do," she said.

In less than an hour, they were parking the truck at the minuscule hangar where Austin and two other local pilots kept their planes. He helped her to board the Cessna, and they pulled on headphones while he did a weather and preflight check. In a matter of minutes, they zoomed down the strip and climbed steeply into the spring afternoon.

The earth receded beneath them, and the slight vibration of the plane was soothing. When they reached 5500 feet, he guided them into the proper heading. The sprawling Mojave appeared beneath them, wrinkled and twisted like a complicated bread loaf ready for baking. She made out the thick runways of Nellis Air Force Base as they kept well away from the restricted airspace.

"Willow's friend Tony used to be stationed there. He flies choppers now and I'd sure like to meet the guy, but he's never around. It's weird."

The panorama was exquisite as they skirted the national park, heading east, but Pilar's attention was drawn to Austin.

Worried as she was about what they might find, she could not help but enjoy the look of unfettered joy on his face. He caught her looking at him.

"What?"

Her cheeks heated. "I forgot how much you love to fly."

He nodded. "Remember that poem you framed for me on my birthday? It's still my favorite, the one by the pilot."

"John Magee."

His expression grew thoughtful. "I understand the last line now."

The last line where the pilot compared flying to touching the face of God. She waited with baited breath for him to continue.

"Used to think the point of flying was to get somewhere." He paused. "I'm beginning to think it's what God reminds me about while I'm up here."

For a moment tears blinded her, and she turned away so he wouldn't see. Austin had changed certainly and so had her feelings for him. She couldn't deny that any longer. But how exactly did she feel about this man with whom she'd once been ready to share her whole life? So much had happened. It was all terribly confusing, her emotions up and down like a plane in turbulence. She might never get it all straightened out, but she was grateful to the Lord to know that Austin was more at peace. Never would she cease to be grateful for that.

They continued on for another hour, mostly in silence, both lost in their thoughts and the acres of wild desert unfolding under them. The needle in the haystack feeling swamped her hopes. She used binoculars to scope out the terrain. Twice he flew closer to observe something she pointed out, with no promising results. "Well," Austin said slowly, "Jude told us to check the area he provided within a hundred-mile radius. We've already swept over most of that twice."

She bit back a groan. What if they found nothing? What if they never learned what had happened to her mother? Panic worked against her lungs.

"I'll make another pass a bit farther out just to be sure," he said.

Below, the land was studded with piñon and mesquite. Through the binoculars, she noticed a piece of land had been cleared and fenced. Large flat depressions were carved into the landscape, giving it the appearance of an alien planet. "What's that down there, Austin?"

"An old copper mine, looks like," he

said. "See that spot there? You can still see some of the graders half-buried in the dirt. Hasn't been used for a long time. There's the road to access it that cuts off from the highway." A long paved stretch still showed relatively free of debris. "Looks like it's closed off to keep out vandals, maybe." His silence told her he was thinking the same thing she was.

What better place to lock someone up? No nosy neighbors to drive by. No one would hear the screams.

"There's a flat area there. I can put the plane down outside the gates," he said slowly. "That wouldn't be trespassing, I don't think. We can look closer, see if there are any signs that someone has been there recently. If so, we can call Jude." He checked the sky. "We have another couple of hours until sunset. A few minutes on the ground won't hurt us. What do you think?"

She looked again out the window. *Mom, are you down there somewhere?* She might as well be a single grain of sand in that vast desert but what if...? What if there was the slightest chance her mother might be down there? Alive? If Max really had imprisoned her, he would pick a place where she couldn't possibly attract attention. Heart beating fast, she nodded to Austin, who began to bring the plane in for a landing.

Pilar's stomach was in knots by the time they deplaned. *Don't get your hopes up. This is one of a million old boarded-up relics.* There were plenty of abandoned mining sites in the desert, and this one looked like all the rest. It had once been a bustling property, no doubt. Some of the land still showed the terracing and flattened basins that marked it as a small-scale operation. The vehicles had been removed, as had any equipment of value. A chain-link fence enclosed the space all the way around. They walked along the perimeter, searching for any signs of recent activity.

"Look at this, Pilar," he said, stopping so suddenly she bumped into him.

She peered at the spot he noted. At first she could see nothing out of the ordinary. Then her skin erupted in goose bumps when she detected the creased metal where the chain link had been bent. "It's been cut and pulled back," she said, voice hushed. "Recently, maybe, since it hasn't had time to form rust on the cut parts."

"Uh-huh," he said. "But to what purpose? We're too far away from any towns for it to be kids out for some troublemaking."

"What about that?" Pilar said. She pointed to a structure they hadn't noticed at first, half buried as it was by drifting sand—a small domed shed, probably for storage. There was only one small window high up in the wood.

She took out the binoculars and trained them on the structure. "Can you message Jude and ask if we can check out the building?"

He tapped a message. They waited for fifteen minutes, meandering up and down the fence line until Pilar's attention was drawn to movement. Again she lifted the binoculars to her eyes.

"Jude said he contacted the property owner and applied some pressure. We..."

But she was no longer listening.

Something fluttered in the light wind, something orange and silky.

Not something, she realized with horror as she dropped the binoculars.

Her mother's scarf.

THIRTEEN

Austin had just finished reading Jude's text—I applied pressure. Landlord says you got five minutes. Then out—when Pilar wrenched back the damaged fencing and took off running. He had no idea what she'd seen, but he was in pursuit in a flash, squeezing through the gap in the fence, yelling at her to stop.

She didn't, until she got to the shed and yanked hard on the door. It didn't open, thanks to the sturdy padlock, which looked suspiciously new and out of place in the long-abandoned work site.

"Wait," he said, stopping her from kicking at it. "What are you doing?"

She pointed to the fluttering orange scrap of fabric flying from the high-up window. "That's my mom's. I gave her that scarf for Mother's Day last year." Her face paled dangerously as she clutched at his hand with fingers gone ice cold. "She's in there, Austin. She put the scarf up there to signal for help."

He texted Jude. Local police would be en route soon. But would soon be soon enough?

"Mom," Pilar yelled, pounding on the door. "Can you hear me?" She pressed her ear to the wood. She almost shrieked. "I hear a groan. She's in there, Austin. She's hurt. We have to get her out."

No more waiting around for help. They had to make something happen now. He hurried along all sides of the shed. "If there was a rear entrance, which I doubt, it's buried under a couple of feet of sand."

She looked as well, coming to the same conclusion. "The window's too small even if you lifted me up."

He examined the door more closely. The metal latch through which the padlock was threaded would be their best chance. "Hang on," he said. He ran to the plane and retrieved the tool kit his father had given him when he first earned his wings at age twenty.

One day, you'll be glad you have these, his father had said, clapping him on the back.

"Boy, were you right, Dad," he muttered, running with the box back to join Pilar. He could hear her breath, shallow and panicky, as she watched him apply a screwdriver under the metal plate. The metal was new and strong, but the wood underneath was not. Age and rot were on his side. He chipped away, bits of the door flying in all directions until the metal began to wobble. One screw popped loose, then the other. The latch and lock fell away. She was pushing to go through when he pulled her back.

"Let me go first."

She pressed her lips together but did not object. He shoved the door open. Inside the shed it was dim, gloomy. He saw the crumpled figure at the same moment Pilar entered behind him.

With a cry, she hurried to her mother, who was lying on her side, back against the wall. Austin had met Bernadette Jefferson before, tall, neatly dressed, elegant. Now she was clad in dirty slacks, her short-sleeve brown shirt torn, exposing a scratched shoulder. Her eyes were closed, and he could not see the rise and fall of her breathing in the darkened room.

Breath held, he knelt next to them.

"Mom," Pilar entreated. Bernadette's eyelids fluttered, and he felt an immense sense of gratitude that they had not been too late. There was a gash on her forehead, and a bruise as if she'd fallen or been struck. A puddle of blood spread out from her hair. An overturned metal trash can lay a foot or so away. He realized what had happened. She'd climbed up on it and managed to shove her scarf through the cracked window. It would have been precarious since her feet and hands were bound with duct tape. The silver tape that circled her wrists was tight. He wondered what kind of man could ever do such a thing to another living person.

"Mom," Pilar whispered. "It's okay. I'm here. Help is on the way."

Austin looked around the dank space. There was a gallon container of water, almost empty and a box of granola bars with one left in the package. Other than that, there was a pile of moldy file folders, some rusted metal gears and a thin blanket, her captor's concession to the cold evening temperatures.

She hadn't been there long enough to starve or die of thirst. Why hadn't Max, or whoever it was, killed her? Why give her barely enough to stay alive? The answer was obvious. She hadn't divulged the information her captor sought, or he'd wanted her living as leverage to force Cyrus to cooperate.

Grimly, he turned his attention back to the stricken woman. "I'll get a first-aid kit. Be right back."

They did their best to staunch the bleeding on her forehead and cut away the duct tape restraints. He suggested they ease a blanket underneath her body to shield her from the cold concrete floor. It was about all they could do without moving her too much.

Pilar applied a moistened gauze to Bernadette's face to cleanse away the dried blood. A water bottle from the plane allowed her to dribble a tiny stream into her mother's parched mouth.

All the while, Pilar's pain was palpable, her anguish and fear killing him an inch at a time.

With a whimper, Bernadette opened her eyes.

Pilar gasped. "Mom, I'm here. You're safe. We're going to get you to a hospital."

"He made me call you," she whispered.

"I didn't want to. He made me tell him there was no Cousin Ellen."

"It's okay, Mom," Pilar said.

Bernadette's mouth worked for a moment before she was able to speak. "Tell Cyrus."

"Tell him what, Mom?" Pilar said, dashing her tears away with her forearm.

"Let Cyrus know, he's coming after him." Tears squeezed from her swollen eyes. She slid back into unconsciousness.

"No, stay with me, Mom. Please." But her mother did not appear to hear.

Pilar talked and prayed and whispered. Austin placed a hand lightly on Pilar's shoulder and prayed along with her. It didn't feel strange to entreat the Lord to help someone in need; it never had. Only for himself could he not seem to ask the Lord's intervention.

Pride, he thought again. His "I can take care of everything myself" mind-set. Well, that certainly had not panned out lately. Pilar in trouble, Ethel missing, shoulder still ruined. As he asked the Lord for grace for Bernadette, it hit him again. The way to grace was humility, and his own heaping helping of pride had kept him from realizing that.

At long last they heard the sound of an ambulance approaching. He added another silent prayer of thanks for the medics who barreled through the broken fencing he'd made sure was open as wide as it would go. A local cop arrived too. Austin was trying his best to explain the sequence of events when a rescue helicopter landed inside the fence. Jude leaped out, startling Austin. He joined them at the shed.

"Got a chopper here in case she needed to be flown to a trauma center. Figured I'd hitch a ride the fastest way I could."

He eyed Pilar, who was kneeling next to a stretcher that just exited the shed. "Status?"

"She's alive. She said to tell my dad

'he's' after him. She was trying to warn him about Max."

"It's a theory."

"More than a theory," Austin said with some heat.

"Still shy of a fact, though. We're going to need some proof before we land on that conclusion."

Austin did not feel the need to do any more fact gathering. It was enough proof in his mind to know Max almost abducted Pilar from his shop and probably fired a flare that nearly resulted in her death. Now finding her mother gravely wounded, imprisoned like an animal? There was no doubt in Austin's mind the "him" was Max. Jude was not waiting for a reply. He walked by Austin and entered the storage shed.

Pilar was still by the side of the stretcher, while the medics prepared her mother for travel. Not wanting to intrude on a private moment, he followed Jude, who stopped him before he entered the shed.

He pointed to a beam that ran along the ceiling.

At first Austin couldn't figure out what Jude was pointing to. Squinting, he finally got it. A small black box, the size of a calculator.

Alarm crept over him. "Is that a...?"

Jude pulled him away a step. "Camera. Looks like it has audio, too, if the batteries are still good."

Austin let that fact sink in slowly, like boots into quicksand. "So everything we said was recorded?"

"Possibly."

The impact settled on him slowly. Bernadette's abductor knew she'd been set free...and no doubt would talk to the police when she recovered. Max, or whoever, now had a narrowing window in which to complete his mission before Bernadette could identify him to the cops. The fuse had well and truly been lit.

"I'll have protection at the hospital," Jude said, as if reading Austin's mind.

But the other fact was more alarming still. The abductor hadn't gotten information about the money stash from Bernadette, since she didn't know Cyrus had hidden it in the old bicycle. With Bernadette in the hospital under police guard, there was only one other person he could use as leverage to get Pilar's dad to confess.

His gaze shot to Pilar.

She was innocent, no idea where this stash of money was kept, just like her mother.

But Max didn't know that.

The only relevant fact for Max was that his very last chance rested in Pilar.

And he was plenty desperate enough to take it.

Pilar was relieved that her mother was flown immediately to the trauma center in Las Vegas, only a half hour from Furnace Falls. Austin could make the flight back to town in less time than that, but they'd had to finish their statement to the local police before they were cleared to go. He took Pilar back to town, where they tended quickly to the dogs and drove directly to the hospital.

The doctor's report was cautiously optimistic. "She'll be monitored closely, but we'll hope that when the swelling goes down and we get her properly hydrated again, she'll recover."

Pilar was not able to control the sobs that escaped her when the doctor excused himself. Austin guided her to a quiet corner and held her while she cried.

"How could he have done it?" she asked through her tears. "How could Max have locked her up and left her there? She must have been terrified. If she hadn't been able to use her scarf...we might... I mean..." He did not let her finish, holding her tightly.

"No what-ifs," he said sternly. "Your mother is going to be okay. She's safe, and Jude and the local police will keep her that way."

But, she realized, the primary problem was still the same. Max wanted his money. "He isn't going to stop until he gets it." She summoned up all the courage she possessed. "I should leave. This is too dangerous for you. You already lost Ethel, and Max will come after me now with both barrels."

He shook her gently. "Pilar, I know I've been pushy in the past, bossy even, but right now I am attempting to put both feet down hard. First of all, the cops haven't completed their search for the money at your apartment complex. Maybe they will find something to lead them to which flea market she took the belongings. They might be able to trace it from there. You should stay in Furnace Falls until we know that much at least. Second, give the police time to examine the camera and the storage shed. Maybe there are some clues that will hint at where Max is holing up. Fourth…"

She summoned a smile. "You forgot third."

"The third one wasn't important." He cupped her cheek, his eyes intense in a way that frightened her. "Fourth, I want to help you finish this, to get your life back."

To get her life back… "There isn't a whole lot to get back to, if Max isn't caught."

He closed the distance between them and kissed her softly on the mouth. Sparks tickled her stomach like fragile flowers ready to bloom. It felt as if a piece of her heart that had long lain dormant started to grow.

"We're going to catch him," Austin said. "I trust my cousin, and I can help keep a look out if you stay here. Just for a few weeks."

Just for a few weeks. That phrase brought her back to reality with a thump.

That was the extent of his invitation. *What did you expect, Pilar? That your ex-fiancé would somehow fall in love with you again?* Of course she hadn't expected that...nor did she want it.

She moved away, straightening her jacket. "I...thank you. I'll stay for a while, until things are more stable with my mom."

"All right." He checked his phone. "It's almost ten. You must be tired. Why don't I take you home for the night?"

"I should stay."

"There is a guard on duty at her door, and the doctor said she's sleeping peacefully. She'd want you to get some rest."

Reluctantly, Pilar followed Austin to the truck. They walked quickly, him holding her elbow. She held back a shiver, the hairs on her neck prickling in the darkness.

Two miles into the drive, Austin stared into the rearview mirror.

She whipped around. "The sedan?"

"Mmm-hmm. Are you buckled up?"

Fear made her voice high. "Yes. Do you think it's Max?"

"Not sure, but it makes sense. He would know we'd have to get your mother to a hospital, and it wouldn't take much to narrow it down to this one, if he listens in on the police scanner frequency. I'm going to try and lose him." He sped up on the quiet highway until he got to the nearest off-ramp. Quickly as he could, he zipped right back on the freeway. The sedan was nowhere in sight. She tried to relax until she spotted the vehicle again when they were almost to Furnace Falls.

"He's back," she said.

"All right." Austin's eyes narrowed. "If he wants to follow, let him. If he thinks he's going to corner us in some isolated area, he's got another thing coming. I haven't chugged a bottle of drugged water this time, Max."

Gripping tightly on the armrests, Pilar could hardly breathe as Austin called the police station. Jude wasn't there, but his second-in-command got on the line. "Bringing you a present," Austin said, explaining quickly.

Five minutes later he drove up a quiet street. With a sudden jerk of the steering wheel, he sailed right into the police parking lot. The sedan hit the brakes once and then squealed around in a tight U-turn and headed away from town. The lights on a parked squad car sprang to life, and the officer pursued the sedan with lights and sirens flashing.

"He'll get him," Pilar said, clutching the seat belt as she watched. "Almost there."

But suddenly an RV rumbled slowly out of the gas station. The inexperienced driver took the turn wide and blocked both lanes. When the driver finally eased his rig out of the way, the sedan was gone. Pilar felt like smacking her fist on the dashboard.

The squad car continued on in search, but her hope died away. The crafty Uncle

Max was slippery as a bar of wet soap. By the time Austin parked the truck at the shop, she could hardly rouse herself to get out. Fatigue and worry about her mother dragged her down and filled her limbs with lead.

Austin helped her from the car and before she knew it, she was sitting in the tiny back room of the shop, accepting licks and love from the dogs. She didn't correct them, even when Waffles tried to slither into her lap. Their warmth dispelled some of the chill, helped the "what-ifs" recede somewhat.

Austin left her for a moment to return with a bologna sandwich, which the dogs sniffed eagerly.

"No, dogs. That's for Pilar."

He went to the back door and turned on the porch light. Security, no doubt, but she knew he was still desperately hoping that Ethel would somehow find her way home. Poor lost dog. Was she suffering out there? Scared? Like Pilar's mom had been? She tried to eat the sandwich. At first it simply would not go down, but after a while her stomach reminded her she was hungry and she polished it off, while Austin did the same to another one he'd made for himself.

The phone in the shop rang.

Austin's eyebrows arched. "Practically no one calls the shop phone, but I figure it's good to have anyway. It's after-hours, so it's probably Aunt Kitty. She never can get the hang of a cell phone."

She toggled Chunk and Lucy on her lap, trying to pet both dogs at once while he answered.

"Hello?" she heard Austin say.

Then silence. His strident tone cleaved the air. "You got some nerve. Isn't it enough that you put your wife and daughter at risk?"

She wriggled free from the dogs and ran to the phone.

He handed it to her, and she held it so they could both hear.

"Where are you, Dad?" she demanded.

"I'm around. I figured I might be able to reach you at Austin's shop, once I found a phone book to look up his number. We didn't finish our talk."

"Dad," she snapped. "We found Mom today."

"What?" His voice cracked. "Where? How is she?"

"She's in the hospital. She was imprisoned in a shed in the middle of an abandoned copper mine. She got a head injury trying to find a way to escape. The doctors think she will pull through if they can get her rehydrated and her head injury heals."

There was dead silence on the other end of the phone.

"Are you there, Dad?"

"Max actually did it." His tone was hard, almost unrecognizable. "He hurt my Birdie."

"We don't know for sure..."

"I do." The words sounded sharp like broken glass.

"She woke for a minute and she told me to tell you something." Pilar repeated the message. "She was worried about you."

There was a moist sniff on the other end, and she realized he was crying.

"My darling Birdie," he said, sniffing. "She was always the stronger of the two of us." He cleared his throat. "It's time for me to step up to the plate. Don't you worry, Peanut. I'm going to finish this. It won't be hard for me to find him."

She exchanged a startled look with Austin. "What are you going to do?"

"Money or no money, I'm going to punish him for what he did to my Birdie, and to you, Pilar."

Alarm bells clanged in her mind. "No, that's not—"

"I have to go, but don't you worry. For once in my life, I'm going to take care of my family. Max is going to pay. If it's the last thing I do, he will not hurt us anymore."

"Dad," she almost shouted, but all she heard in reply was the dial tone.

FOURTEEN

Two days dragged on.

Austin worried about Pilar. He had to press her to eat anything, and the shadows under her eyes indicated the lack of sleep was wearing on her. She jumped every time the phone rang or a customer came to the door of the shop. There had been no word from the police or her father. Jude tried to reassure them that Cyrus might have a hard time tracking down Max despite his boasts, to enact whatever plan he'd concocted to stop him. Somehow, Austin didn't think so. Furnace Falls was a small town and Max was eager to find Cyrus, as well. The two planets would collide at some point.

Laney was still on bed rest.

"Climbing the walls," Beckett informed him. "Aunt Kitty had to hide her cell phone to keep her from calling the hotel every hour or two."

Austin had put hundreds of miles on his truck driving Pilar back and forth to the hospital. On every trip, he'd scoured the roadsides, searching for Ethel. His calls to every local shelter had produced no results. After so much time, there was not much chance of finding her alive, but he tried not to think about that.

Wednesday afternoon, his phone buzzed with a request from his sister.

It's delivery day and Herm and I are swamped. Can you come?

Pilar quickly agreed. "It will be good to do something besides pace the floor and pet the dogs."

In the Hotsprings loading area, Austin checked for any signs of Max or his vehicle, but there weren't any. The four of them hauled boxes from the van to the kitchen. Trying to keep his mortification at a reasonable level, he used a handcart to ease the strain on his shoulder for the heavy pallets of potatoes and meat. Time to be a man and accept help when he needed it. Still, it gave him a pang to remember how he used to be able to move entire crates of tools into his shop with ease.

Someday I'll...

He stopped. No more of that. *Why don't you try and be grateful that you can help, even if it's not the same way as before?* He found the thought cleared away his discomfort, at least for the moment. They finished, and Herm started in at once on some sort of vegetable stock. Pilar and Willow washed and trimmed strawberries in a massive colander.

Austin popped his head in to check the reception room. "Still not painted," he said as he strolled back into the kitchen. "Beckett is going to throw a fit."

"Not as big a fit as Laney." Willow slit open a ten-pound bag of sugar and re-filled the canister. "I'm going to grab Gary next time I see him and tell him to rearrange the priority list to get that room painted if he knows what's good for him."

Austin figured Levi wouldn't care one whit about the color of the reception room as long as he got to marry Mara. The way they looked at each other...had he gazed at Pilar like that when they'd been engaged? He watched her now, her movements graceful, quietly listening to his sister's persistent chatter. If he didn't know Pilar, what would he think of her by what he saw now?

She was a generous helper.

Someone who struggled with decisions, trying to find the one right answer when there wasn't one.

Content to let others take the spotlight.

Patient.

Quietly stubborn.

Ill at ease, sometimes.

Perfect.

No, he told himself. She wasn't perfect. Then why did she seem a perfect match for him?

I've got to stop. To keep himself busy, he grabbed a broom and swept the dining room while Pilar finished her work with the berries.

They decided to take a break in the courtyard, sitting under the shade of an enormous twisted pine to cool down before the ride back to the shop. She checked on her mother with a quick hospital phone call. Her knee bobbed with nervous energy. He felt the same. With so many balls in the air that could come crashing down any moment, he wasn't sure which one to focus on. All were important, but nothing rolled through his mind with as much impact as the fact that Pilar's mom was improving and the clock was ticking down until Pilar would insist on leaving, no matter how many reasons to stay he brought up.

And why should that stick inside him like a piece of swallowed glass? She was his ex-fiancée, emphasis on the *ex*, and two weeks ago he would have reversed course on the sidewalk to avoid seeing her. What had changed? Nothing, he told himself, except a little maturing on his part. They didn't have to be enemies. It was better they parted as friends.

But the truth was, he didn't want to think about them parting at all.

He was grateful when her phone rang, hauling him from his unruly musings. She put it on speakerphone, and he leaned close to hear, trying not to inhale the clean scent of the shampoo she'd used that morning.

"It's Jude. I heard back from Cliffton police. They finished searching your apartment."

Pilar's excitement bubbled up into an enticing pink sheen on her cheeks. "Did they find—" she looked around suddenly, cautious "—anything?"

"No, nothing out of the ordinary. Definitely no bike and no indication where the storage unit contents were taken. They did remove boxes of old paperwork. I'm going to get there at some point and help my buddy go through it. Slim chance it could lead to the flea market where the bike was sold."

Pilar sagged, and he instinctively put a hand on her knee.

"Nothing at all?" she said. "I guess it was too much to hope for."

Jude was quiet for a moment. "I don't mean to offend, but it's possible that your mother did find the money in the bike, and she's got it stashed in the apartment somewhere we didn't stumble across."

"My mother isn't a liar." Then her face colored. He knew she was thinking of the lie her mother had told about her father being dead.

Jude didn't reply for a moment. "We

need to cover all the bases before we decide for sure the money is gone."

Pilar sighed and thanked Jude before clicking off. "Bad to worse," she said.

"You gotta go slow to go fast, right?" he replied. "At least we know where it isn't."

Pilar shook her head. "I don't believe my mom would have lied about hiding the money if she had found it. Then again... I might be wrong. Do you think...?"

He waited patiently.

She chewed her lip. "Do you think the cops might have missed something?"

"Possible." He thought it over. "I've got an idea. How about we fly over there? Would only take about an hour or so. You can go through the place and double-check. I'll help. Four eyes are better than two and all that."

Her face brightened. "Wow. Two flights in one week? How did I get so fortunate?"

He winked at her. "Helps to know people."

She laughed in that high, floaty delicate way that reminded him of Christmas bells. "All right. I guess it's a way to pass the time if nothing else. I'm ready for takeoff any time, Captain. When should we go?"

"As much as I'd like to say 'right now,' I have a bunch of orders I really need to complete today at the shop, and I know you want to drive back and see your mom tomorrow morning. How about after that?"

"Do you really think we might find something that could end this?"

"Won't know until we try, right? Maybe there's an old bike stuck in the rafters or something."

She flung her arms around his neck, which thrilled him more than it should have. He resisted the urge to kiss the soft cheek pressed next to his.

"Thank you, Austin. You didn't need to do any of this for me. It's very generous."

Generous. He liked that word. It wasn't a term he would have applied to himself, but it thrilled him to know she thought that about him.

The back door to the kitchen swung shut and Gary shuffled out, his overalls splotched with paint. He was eating a piece of toast spread with the fresh fig preserves Herm produced. He gave them a wave and disappeared rapidly around the corner.

Willow followed a few moments later. "Where did Gary go? I was trying to tell him about getting the reception room done, but I turned around and he was gone."

"He was probably trying to escape your clutches," Austin said. "I can't think why."

She gave him a sassy look. "Ha-ha. Well, guess who is going to be frantically painting if he doesn't get it done in time, brother dear?"

Austin shrugged. "I should have given Gary a pep talk."

Willow raised an eyebrow, glancing

from Austin to Pilar. "What are you two plotting?"

"Plotting?" Austin raised an innocent brow.

"Yeah. You look like you have a secret. I'm nervous about you two after all that's gone on around here lately." She cocked her head. "And you have that gleam of excitement in your eye, Austin. What gives?"

"We have to run, actually," he said, getting up from his chair and giving her a kiss, "but don't worry. If we have a big secret to share, you'll be the first to know, I promise."

She gave him that look, the one that she'd used to skewer him since they were children and then pulled him in for a hug. "Do you know what you're doing, little brother?" she whispered in his ear.

He realized by her tone she was talking about his relationship with Pilar, not their secretive plans. She must have seen them hugging through the kitchen window and figured out it sent him into confused circles of thought. Was he acting differently? Was it apparent to everyone that his feelings were a jumbled mess? Returning the hug, he stepped away.

"Of course I know what I'm doing," he said, while his heart vigorously disagreed.

His brain said, *Search the apartment, solve Pilar's problems,* but his heart whispered something entirely different. Shutting out the clamor, he called Jude to tell him of their plans.

Pilar ignored Austin's protest and swept the shop, tidied piles of invoices and exercised the dogs. If she didn't keep busy, she might just explode. She kept thinking of her father. Why should she be so gravely worried about his actions? He'd never been much of a dad to her. Her family life was wrapped in layers of lies and disappointments.

But couldn't she chalk up plenty of

moral failures in her own past? Leaving Austin, for one. She thought about his self-improvement list and smiled in spite of her worry. If she wanted to be forgiven, she had to forgive, and that meant letting go of the burning anger she felt toward her father.

"All right, Lord," she said quietly. She asked His help in extending forgiveness toward both her parents for their duplicity, and also entreated Him to intervene before her father could get hurt or commit murder.

The prayers stayed in her heart, and she actually managed to sleep for a few hours here and there until the morning sun finally made an appearance. After a quick breakfast, they were on the road to Las Vegas.

At the hospital, there were encouraging signs from her mother. The swelling had gone down in her face, and she was no longer wearing an oxygen mask to aid her breathing. She even stirred once or twice and opened her eyes for a brief moment.

"Mom," Pilar said, heart in her throat. "Are you waking up?"

Her mother did not come to full consciousness, but Pilar was certain when she pressed her mother's hand she got a faint return squeeze. It was enough to buoy her spirits. The guard on the way out assured them that no one had attempted to see Bernadette.

He pointed to a hallway camera. "Aside from a guard at the door, there's a camera right there and a security station around the corner. No one would be able to get in here without being seen and stopped."

She thanked him profusely.

Austin hustled her to the truck again, and they were on their way straight to the airstrip. Though she knew the chance of them finding a clue the police had missed was slim to none, excitement rippled through her. He sensed her mood and gave her that smile, the one that pulled the blue from his eyes and lent them a sapphire hue.

"Thanks again for taking me," Pilar said, the words suddenly stumbling over her tongue.

"My honor," he said. "It would be a coup if we found some indication of where that money wound up."

She could never compete with Austin's enormous optimism. Her own sense of caution and worry would not allow it. Still, she was happy that their breakup and the trauma she'd brought into his life since he'd shown up on her doorstep with Chunk had not stripped away all of his cheerful inclination. He'd regained it somehow, in spite of his injury. Something else to be grateful for.

They parked at the airstrip. The noon sunshine was blinding as they walked to the hangar.

"Are you whistling?" she said, marveling.

"Uh, yeah. Guilty. I feel cheerful, but

maybe I shouldn't with everything going on. I mean, your mom's doing better and we get to fly again today."

She reached for his hand. "It's good to see you that way, Austin." And it was so lovely there in the sunlight with not a cloud in the vast blue sky, her hand in his. If it was only for a moment, she would let herself enjoy it. Now that was a page from the Austin Duke playbook.

His grip tightened. "Pilar, where did that car come from?"

She followed his gaze to a vehicle stopped fifty yards away from the hangar. It was not the sedan she'd grown accustomed to looking for, but a dented blue Honda. They both froze. The door opened, as if someone was ready to get out.

"Does it belong to another pilot?" she said.

That question was answered when the door suddenly slammed shut again and the engine was cranked to life. With a squeal of tires, the Honda exploded toward them. Austin looked around wildly, and Pilar realized their plight. They were halfway between the hangar and the truck. Which should they run for?

They both came to the same conclusion and began to sprint back to the truck. Austin was fumbling in his pocket for the keys. Behind them the Honda was gaining ground, now only fifty feet behind, now forty, thirty.

Her lungs burned as she tried to keep up with Austin's long-legged stride. As she began to drop back behind him, he slowed, took her arm and towed her alongside him.

Risking a glance behind, she found the front bumper was now only a matter of feet, the windshield so blinding in the sunlight she could not see the driver's face. Max? Had he gotten another car? Stolen one? The ground shook as they ran. The truck was so near. With only a few strides to go, Austin lost his grip on the keys. They flew from his fingers and momentum carried them forward. There was no way to retrieve them without being crushed by the pursuing vehicle.

At first she did not understand until he tugged her in front of him and yanked her arm downward. She got it, dropped to her knees and crawled under the body of the truck.

"Austin," she shouted as the vehicle bore down on them at full speed.

He rolled under a second before the Honda rammed into the passenger door. A roar of collapsing metal and breaking glass drowned out her scream. Austin wrapped his arms around her and twisted his body to be on the impact side. The force of the crash was great, but the Honda was not a heavy enough vehicle to crush the truck. The frame rocked with the onslaught.

Her breathing came in pants and gasps,

cheek pressed to the asphalt. They'd survived. They'd not been crushed.

Her relief was fleeting as she realized the driver had forced his vehicle into Reverse and once again floored the accelerator to finish what he'd started.

FIFTEEN

Austin's mind raced for ideas, but he couldn't latch on to anything except to drag his cell phone from his pocket and frantically punch in 911. No time for a message before the Honda was accelerating for another smash, but maybe the cops could track Austin's location.

One wheel had already exploded from the first impact, and it lay in shreds around them. The truck was tough, but another blow would probably collapse the frame to the point where they would be exposed. What could he do? The area around the airstrip was flat acres of grass, no trees even to offer shelter. There was nowhere to run, and no time to get there.

The car was so close fragments of

gravel were flying around and striking them. His own helplessness was infuriating. All he could do was push Pilar deeper under the chassis and make sure his body would absorb most of the impact and flying glass. He tried to at least identify the driver, but the angles were all wrong for that.

"Hold on, Pilar," he yelled, as the Honda closed in again. He readied for the crash, jaw gritted and one boot braced on the rear tire. Three, two...

Nothing. The Honda abruptly broke off, speeding down the airstrip. Wiping the grit from his eyes, he tried to make sense of it. With a jerk of the wheel, the car left the paved strip, bumped across a section of grass and made for the dirt access road.

In a moment it was out of view. The sound of his pulse still roared in Austin's ears as he tried to steady his breathing.

Pilar was still rigid with terror. "What happened?"

He began to wriggle from underneath. "He saw someone else coming and it scared him off." The familiar green Jeep raced into view. "It's Trevor. He's one of the other two pilots who share the hangar with me."

He crawled out from under the truck and was helping Pilar when Trevor jammed his car to a stop and ran over. "I saw the crash. What is going on? Should I call an ambulance?"

"No," Austin said after checking with Pilar. Her forehead was streaked with dirt, and bits of glass glittered in her sweater. "I called 911, but I didn't give them any information. They—"

Trevor pointed to two speeding police cars careening in their direction. "I guess they figured it out. Who was that guy?"

"It's a long story. Do you mind if Pilar sits in your car for a minute?" He did not want to have her walk the distance to the hangar after what she'd endured.

Pilar didn't protest. Her legs were trembling so much she could not hide it. He led her to Trevor's back seat and knelt next to her as she sank into it. For a moment he rested his forehead on her knee, and she caressed his hair. The moment hung in time, drawn out and surreal.

While the cops approached across the tarmac, they watched, breathing deeply.

The narrowness of their escape rattled him. He closed his eyes and squeezed their clasped hands. Should he have anticipated such an attack? But who would have guessed they'd be at the airstrip again? His mind spun in helpless circles until he realized she'd lain her head on top of his.

"I'm sorry," she whispered. "Now your truck is ruined again because of me."

He freed himself and cupped her chin. "My truck is not important. You are safe and that's all that matters."

"No, it's not," she said miserably. "This gets worse and worse. It's an endless nightmare."

"It's not going to be endless," he said, wiping the tears that rolled down her cheeks. "We aren't out of options."

She shook her head. "I know what you're thinking. We should go to the apartment, like we planned."

"Might be the way to end things, especially if we did find a clue to where the money went. Either way, we'd know we've done all we could."

"I'm afraid that's a waste of time. The money is probably long gone."

Their conversation was interrupted by the medics and police. The next hour was a whirlwind of answering questions, calling Jude, arranging to borrow the truck from Levi yet again. By the time they drove back to his shop, she was deep in thought and nearly silent. He didn't want to push her, figuring she'd tell him when she'd decided about the flight. He drove slowly, window rolled down to catch the breeze.

"I just want to do the right thing," she

318 Death Valley Double Cross

said suddenly when they were a block from the shop. "Not the selfish thing."

"You wouldn't do the selfish thing," he said. "It's not in you."

"Oh, how can you say that?" she snapped. "I left you, Austin. I thought about myself and my family and yes, I was worried about you too, but I left you. Doesn't get much more selfish than that."

"And I left you too," he shot right back.

She frowned. "What?"

"I went into a depression after my injury and I shut you out, pushed you away and made it clear I didn't need you. You physically left, I emotionally left, as my sister would put it. So where does that leave us?" He gripped the steering wheel in frustration. "We've both made wrong choices and we've both learned. What's happening right now isn't about the past, it's about securing your future."

Again she lapsed into silence, brow furrowed in confusion. He wondered if he had shared too much, spoken before he'd had a chance to fully ponder the issue. But he knew it was the truth; he had left her, in a way. And how could he blame her for doing the same thing while trying to protect him?

He pulled into his parking place next to the shop. As soon as he opened the door, he knew something was desperately wrong. The dogs were barking a full on hysterical chorus, and it was not their usual welcoming song.

"Let me check the building," he said, leaving Pilar in the truck with her finger on the 911 button and running to the door. He reached for the handle, stopping before he touched it. The door was unlocked, the bolt scratched where it had been picked. Was Max lying in wait inside? Thinking of the poor dog he'd lost the last time Max showed up made him grind his teeth together. He should walk away and leave it to the police, but he could not stand the thought that another one of his dogs might be hurt or in danger. Quickly he texted Jude.

Instead of the front entrance, he raced around the back and let himself in the gate, relieved to see the dogs. They barked, their tails erect and agitation evident in the elevated scruff along their necks. At least all three were still there, unharmed as far as he could tell.

He went to the rear and peered in through the tiny window just to the side of the bark-o-lounger. Nothing amiss that he could see until...

Horror swept through him as he fixed on something white, visible around the edge of the couch. A hand protruded just far enough for him to see. It was limp, fingers splayed. Clearly a male hand.

But whose?

Then he realized the door was slightly ajar. Tapping it with his toe sent it creaking open. He wouldn't go in, but he had to know.

Who was the man on the floor? Did he need medical attention?

Or not?

Breath held, he leaned over the threshold, bracing himself against for what he might find.

Pilar waited in the locked truck, skin prickled with goose bumps in spite of the afternoon warmth. She checked her phone again. Austin had been gone ten minutes.

I'm okay. Dogs are too. Need to wait here. Stay put, his text had read.

Her questioning follow-up messages had gone unanswered. With each passing minute, her anxiety ballooned. She was ready to charge the backyard and find out for herself what was going on when Jude rolled up, lights flashing. He acknowledged her with a simple nod and hurried around the back.

What could have happened? Why couldn't Austin rejoin her at the truck?

Another interminable ten minutes went by until Jude and Austin appeared together around the side. She rolled opened the door and hopped out, a question on her lips.

Jude beat her to it. "Need to get my team in here. You two will have to stay outside for now. This is gonna take a few hours. Maybe head over to Levi's." Austin looked miserably from Jude to her, but he didn't quite meet her eyes.

"Are you going to tell me?" she said.

Jude blew out a breath. "There's been a murder."

Murder? Her throat closed up. Terror twisted her nerves into knots.

"We need you to take a look at something. Can you?" Jude asked.

Could she?

"One minute. No longer." He gestured for her to follow him.

Dumbly, Pilar took Austin's offered hand and trailed Jude to the back, wading in a daze through the flustered dogs.

There was a sheet-covered body on the floor near the bark-o-lounger. Her stomach heaved. Jude stopped her at the bottom of the porch steps.

"It's Max," he said. "He's been strangled."

Time stopped. Max? Dead? Murdered?

She would have faltered if Austin's other hand hadn't been at the small of her back. What should she feel? She didn't know. But there was something else. Jude did not need her to identify Max, so why had she been brought here?

The question must have been clear to Jude, because he pointed to a small item on the floor she hadn't even noticed. He cleared his throat. "Do you recognize this?"

She leaned close to look at the banged-up leather billfold with the inexpertly embossed letters. And in a moment she was a nine-year-old child again, watching her father open the present she had laboriously made for him in summer camp.

Daddy, with love, Pilar.

"It's Dad's," she said, stunned. "I gave it to him when I was a child."

He nodded. "Okay."

She looked in horror at Jude. "You think my dad did this."

"I don't have any conclusions yet. The wallet is circumstantial evidence, but you told me he said on the phone he was going to find Max and end his threats."

"But that was just talk, he wouldn't…" She trailed off. What wouldn't her father do? He'd stayed in jail all those years and kept quiet about his stolen money, left his daughter and wife to struggle without him. Did she even know what her father would or wouldn't do?

Without another word she turned and left the yard. In the front, she sat on a brick retaining wall.

Austin joined her. "Why don't we go over to Levi's? We can wash up and wait for Jude to finish here."

She tried to answer, but the words caught in her throat.

"Pilar, tell me what you're thinking. Please."

"I think it's time for me to go home."

"Home?"

"To the apartment."

He cocked his head. "You want to search for the money?"

"No." Pain rose like a desert wind through her sinking spirits. "There's no more reason to search for anything. Max is dead and my father…" She swallowed hard. "It looks like he will be going to prison again, this time for murder."

"We don't know that yet. The wallet could have been stolen…planted there…" He paused. "If it was Max at the airstrip trying to run us down, why would he have come immediately to the shop afterward? And how would your father have known he'd show up there?"

All she could think of was that wallet. She wished she could bolt, sprint into the hills and run until the terrible feelings drained away. "I have to prepare the apartment for Mom's release," she said dully. "We have no other place to go."

Austin leaned forward to take her hand, but she snatched it out of his grasp. "I should have never come back, Austin. A runaway bride was bad enough, but this..." She felt her insides turning to stone. "My mother lied to me. My father is a robber and—" she forced it out "—and likely a murderer."

"I don't care about those things—" he started.

"Well, you should." Now she was on her feet. "My family is a wreck, and I guess I am too."

He faced her, head-on. "When I felt useless, I pushed you away, and everyone else I loved. Don't make that same mistake, Pilar. Don't push me away when you need me the most."

Needed him? At that moment, she

had no idea what she needed. Even God seemed so very far away. She dissolved into sobs, and he took her in his arms. She should not let him, but she did. Still deep down she knew the best thing for him was for her to leave and never come back. How would she ever convince her heart to do it?

Numb and anguished, she allowed him to take her to the ranch. She washed her scratched cheeks and dirty hands in the bathroom of the main house. Her reflection seemed strange, her haggard face belonging to someone she didn't recognize. In a stupor, she donned a borrowed T-shirt that hung down over her torn jeans. Outside, she wandered to the pasture fence to see the horses. Instinctively, she looked over her shoulder before she reminded herself. No more need to be afraid. Max was dead. There was no one waiting to snatch her anymore, stalking her every move.

She felt sadness, instead of relief. Austin stood on the porch, watching. She had no idea what she should do. Stay or go? There really was no reason to remain in the shop any longer. Her mother was almost ready to be released. The truth was, she desperately did not want to leave Austin, but what was there in it for him if she stayed? Friendship? Certainly nothing more. And a town full of people who could now add "daughter of a murderer" to the "runaway bride" identity.

Her phone rang with a hospital number. She snatched it up.

"This is a nurse from Las Vegas Hospital," a voice said.

"Is my mom...?" she said in a strangled tone that brought Austin to her side.

"Your mom is fine," the nurse hurried to add. "As a matter of fact, she apparently awakened and asked the orderly for a notepad. She wrote a message for you before she went back to sleep."

"A message? What did it say?"

The nurse read it out. "'Not him.'"

Pilar's mouth hung open. "Is...is that it?"

"Yes, ma'am. Does it make sense to you?"

Sense? She hardly thought so. Nothing had made sense to her since the day she ran from that church and away from her life with Austin. "Uh, thank you," she said. "I appreciate it."

The nurse confirmed her mother was due to be released early the following week. She disconnected.

Austin quirked an eyebrow. "Your mom left you a message?"

She nodded and repeated it back to him. "I have no idea what it means."

They stood in silence for a while, watching the horses crop the grass, tails swishing gracefully.

"What do you want to do, Pilar?"

"I guess I should go home. The doctor said Mom will need a supply of special foods until she's well, and I want to clean up the place after the police searched."

"Would you like me to fly you there and help?"

She searched his face for reluctance, repugnance about what he'd learned of her kin, frustration at her wishy-washy decision-making. She saw nothing but tenderness and an unfamiliar patience.

"Yes. Please."

He smiled. "We can't get back into my shop for a while anyway. Wheels up in a half hour?"

She nodded. She would go and prepare for her mother's homecoming, but there was no guarantee she would be coming back with Austin to Furnace Falls. A deep pain carved its way into her chest as she followed him, and they drove away from the Rocking Horse Ranch.

SIXTEEN

There was none of the joy in their earlier flight on this journey.

"Thanks for the ride," Jude said from his squished jump seat in the rear of the plane. "I'm going to lend a hand looking through those papers taken from the apartment in the search. The flight will save me boatloads of time."

He pulled his cap over his brow and promptly went to sleep.

Pilar was alternately quiet, or sniffly with tears. Though he reached out to squeeze her hand, she avoided contact, jammed as far away as she could get from him in the small plane cockpit.

For the first time, he truly understood what it must have felt like for her when he shoved her away. Sure, he'd done it with a grim smile, hiding behind biting humor, but he realized it must have been agonizing not to be able to comfort the one she loved.

Loved? The irony was almost too much. Now, the moment he'd allowed himself to acknowledge that he was once again in love with Pilar, was the moment she'd pulled away completely. Was this God telling him they were not meant to be together? He wanted to think about it, pray about it, but the flight was a short one and soon they were taxiing onto a small private runway.

A police car picked Jude up at the airstrip. He and Pilar waited for an Uber in silence. What was supposed to happen here? He would go and help her and then what? Would she fly back to Furnace Falls with him? Her expression was stricken, and it cut him to the core.

"You're not going to come back with me, are you?" he said.

She swallowed, the muscles in her throat convulsing. "Please don't ask me that right now. I don't know what the right answer is." There was despair in her voice.

Austin was the type of guy who always figured he knew what was right. Snap decisions, everything would work out somehow. And Pilar was the other end of the spectrum, a woman who worried deeply about making the right decision, fearing that her emotions would spur her to a reckless choice. He could imagine how she would have wrestled over leaving the church that fateful day in September.

"Sometimes," he said softly, "I think maybe God leads us by the feelings He gives us here." He tapped his chest.

"What are you feeling, Austin?"

"That you are in a terrible mindset right now, that you should come back with me, let me take care of you for a while." He added a cheeky grin in case his emotions were too heavily applied. "A bunch of dog kisses are the best medicine for any ailment."

She met his gaze then, her own eyes shining with unshed tears. "Please..." she said. "I can't answer you right now. I'm sorry."

He nodded, but he thought he saw an indication of what her future answer would be. He swallowed as the Uber came and whisked them away to her apartment. She inserted the key with shaking fingers, and they went in.

He'd only gotten a vague impression of the place when he'd arrived with Chunk. How long ago that seemed. The tiny front room was dark, the curtains still drawn. They went down the hallway to the cramped kitchen where there were still dishes in the sink, left from before he'd shown up on her doorstep. The cops had no doubt been thorough in their search, going through the cupboards, the drawers, but there was plenty left to tidy up.

"I'm going to go put fresh linens on Mom's bed."

"Okay. I'll fix up the kitchen."

Pilar disappeared down the hallway. He considered the dishes in the sink and set to work. Pilar's mom's strange message floated into his mind. *Not him.* Not who? Not Max? But if the man who'd abducted her wasn't Max, who was it? His phone buzzed with a message so he dried his hands. He was about to pull it out when he heard Pilar scream.

Bolting down the hallway he slammed through the bedroom door.

Pilar was not alone.

Her father stood near the bed, ghastly pale against the drawn curtains. He stood there with his palms up. Austin edged in next to Pilar.

"What do you want, Cyrus?"

"I had to talk to my daughter."

"Dad," Pilar cried, tortured. "How can you come back here looking for me after what you've done? You didn't have to kill

Max." Her voice broke. Austin put a protective arm around her. He didn't think Cyrus would hurt his daughter, but he wasn't taking any chances.

Cyrus's eyes bulged. "Kill him? I didn't kill anyone. I didn't even know he was dead."

Austin frowned. "He was strangled at my shop with your wallet nearby."

"Don't lie anymore, Dad. Please," Pilar begged.

"You have to turn yourself in," Austin said. "At least give Pilar that. Show her you can do what's right, for her sake."

Cyrus shoved a hand through his unkempt hair, sending in into further disarray. "I know you aren't going to believe me, but I didn't kill Max. He stole my wallet from the campsite along with my phone. I'm not lying."

Her face went white. "How can I believe what you say? You've lied all these years, keeping the money a secret. Mom lied about you being in prison."

"Only to protect me. Don't blame her. I didn't give her the life she deserved."

"So how did you know to find us here?"

"I figured you'd show up eventually with Birdie, and I wanted to talk to you both before…"

Pilar shook her head. "Before you disappeared permanently?"

He hung his head. "I was going to get far enough away where I wouldn't be caught before I sent for you. But now I'll be blamed for Max's murder. The cops will never believe me."

Pilar's eyes blazed. "You need to stand up and face what you did."

Austin's phone buzzed again. He flicked a look. At first he didn't understand.

"'Pete Silvers doesn't have a sister,'" he said, reading Jude's message aloud. "What…?"

Pilar cocked her head. "Pete Silvers, the armored car guard," she mused aloud. "He told Jude that Max bought coffee from his sister's shop, remember?"

Austin watched as the second message appeared. "Jude says Pete's been in Furnace Falls, disguising himself as a painter at—"

"The Hotsprings," Pilar interrupted, horrified. "Gary the painter. That's why the work wasn't getting done. He was there to get information about the money."

Mind spinning, Austin relayed Jude's next message. "'His fingerprints were on the lock on the storage shed. Stay put.'"

Cyrus's mouth fell open. "Pete was the one who locked up Birdie? Killed Max?"

"Why shouldn't I?" They all jerked to find Pete Silvers holding a gun on them from the doorway. His expression was so vicious, he was almost unrecognizable from the chatty painter. "You took everything from me, Cyrus. I'm owed something. That money should be mine. I know you told your wife where it was, but she wouldn't tell me."

"You imprisoned her," Cyrus whispered.

"Not like you ever stayed around to protect her," Pete said, sneering.

Cyrus's nostrils flared.

Austin spoke quickly, hoping to distract Cyrus from doing something dumb. "It was you driving the car at the airstrip."

"Yeah. Overheard your plans to come here. Gotta love a speakerphone." His smile was terrifying. "Told you my back was no good for painting, or anything else, thanks to Daddy Dearest, here. So where's the money?"

"There isn't any," Pilar said. "It was in a storage unit and my mom didn't know. She sold the contents."

"Nice try. Your mother made up that story. I heard you two discussing the whole storage unit thing at the Hotsprings."

"It's not a story," Pilar started. "It's—"

"Oh, it's here, otherwise you three wouldn't be," Pete said, cutting her off. "And I want to know where."

Austin wanted to push Pilar behind him,

but Pete was standing between them. "Let them go and I'll help you look," he said.

"Right," he said, a smirk on his face. "That'd be a smart idea." He gestured with the gun. "I'm not a very practiced shot. I took this off Max's body after I strangled him. Busy day really. After I tried to stop you two from flying off to the apartment, I was driving back through town and who do I see but Max, sneaking into the shop? I was tired of his getting in between me and my money, so I killed him and imagine my surprise to find Cyrus's wallet in his pocket. Serendipity. Figured with Cyrus in jail for the murder, it would be clear sailing. I could arrange another drugged water bottle or something to take care of you and mum and find the money myself. But you've gone and messed that up, all of you. I can still tie you all up after I get what's mine and leave, but if you don't cooperate, I'll kill you instead. Might take me a few shots to get the job done, but I don't think I can miss too badly at this range."

Austin moved forward, hands loose at his sides. Pete could start shooting at any moment. He had to get him to move away from Pilar and Cyrus.

"I was searching the kitchen when you came in," he said. "I might have found something."

Pete's eyes narrowed. "Why don't you go check that out, flyboy?" He grabbed Pilar by the sleeve and pulled her tight to his side. "She can stay here with me."

Pilar winced at his hard grip. Her pain ignited something in Cyrus.

"You won't hurt my daughter, like you did my wife," he shouted, face suffused with scarlet rage. He lowered his head and charged.

"No, Dad," Pilar screamed.

Pete flung Pilar aside and fired wildly. Cyrus grunted in pain and fell to his knees. Pete's second shot punched a hole in the bedroom window. The third struck something in the hallway with a sound of shattering glass. Austin grabbed Pilar's wrist and pulled her to the door. She stumbled, crying out in pain as her ankle gave way. He yanked her up and kept going.

"Dad," she cried, but he would not let her return. The back door was their best avenue of escape. A bullet exploded behind them. Austin pushed Pilar into the kitchen and grabbed a chair in one fluid movement. As soon as Pete passed the threshold, he whirled the chair around in an arc.

It made contact with Pete's arm, knocking the gun loose. Austin did not see where it landed, nor did he care. Now he aimed a punch that caught Pete in the stomach. He doubled over but did not go down. Austin felt his shoulder go numb as Pete recovered, straightening. The gun was on the floor where it had come to rest in the corner.

With his shoulder useless, he aimed a

powerful kick at Pete's knee, but the blow was poorly aimed. Pete was inches from the gun when Pilar emerged from under the table and snatched up a pan from the cupboard. She swung and made contact with his elbow.

He roared in pain, but still crawled toward the discarded gun.

Suddenly, Jude exploded through the back kitchen door, gun drawn, a second officer at his side.

"Stop right there," he yelled at Pete. There was a sound of the front door being battered open. "Police," a voice yelled, as more cops advanced through the front door.

Groaning, Pete stopped and held up his hands. "I shouldn't be the one going to jail," he said, face contorted with hatred. "I deserve justice."

"Trust me, you'll get what you deserve," Jude said, keeping his gun trained steadily on Pete as the other officer handcuffed him.

"'Bout time you got here," Austin quipped.

"Sorry," Jude said with an eye roll. "Traffic. I sent you some texts, you know."

"I know," Austin said. "I could hardly believe it."

Pilar hobbled toward the bedroom. Austin tried to stop her, but she pulled up short as an officer led her father out of the bedroom into the hallway. Cyrus had a trickle of blood coming from his biceps.

"Hey, Peanut. Good thing he was telling the truth about being a bad shot."

With a cry she embraced him. Cyrus's expression was tender, pained and uncertain all rolled into one, but he hugged his daughter with such joy that Austin did not doubt he loved her.

"What's going to happen?" Pilar said as she released him. Austin watched Cyrus straighten with surprise as he looked over her shoulder.

He laughed, a hearty booming chuckle. "Well, Peanut. I guess I'm going to jail again for a while." He grinned and pointed. "On the upside, it looks like Mom's craft projects are worth more than she thought."

They turned to look at the white framed, twin mirrors on the wall. One had shattered, bits of glass falling from the frame, which looked very odd. A chunk of it had been blown away, revealing a blackened interior.

"Mom's a big proponent of repurposing," she said, wonder lighting her face. "Do those frames look like they used to be something else?"

Austin still didn't get it. He peered closer. What had seemed to be the knobs and whorls of a wooden painted frame, now materialized into something very familiar indeed. "A bicycle tire."

"Two of them." Jude stepped closer, staring at the matching mirror frames. He poked a pen inside the damaged one. "There are bills in here concealed behind black plastic, tacked to the rubber tire."

"I did a good job hiding them, didn't I?"

Cyrus said, grinning. "Your mom probably never even noticed when she put a mirror inside and spray painted the tread white. She must have figured that was some pretty heavy rubber." He whistled. "Birdie always did have a way of seeing things in a new way. Leave it to her to make frames out of bicycle tires."

Pilar's expression softened and she started to laugh.

He was still lost in the discovery. Right here, the money that had caused so much trouble and even a murder, had been hanging on the apartment wall the whole time.

Now Austin joined in the laughter, reveling in the fact that, at long last, Pilar would be safe and have the future she deserved.

Pilar didn't imagine a badly sprained ankle could hurt so much, but the pain was persistent enough that she could not fall asleep. Willow had checked on her repeatedly, at one point flopping down in frustration, saying, "Would you please tell my brother to go home already? The dogs are waiting for him, and he's getting on my last nerve asking me how you are every five minutes. Beckett will have his ears if he drives away any guests by patrolling the hallway."

Sleep had found her somehow for a few hours before dawn. Now, awaking the next morning in the Hotsprings Hotel, she took in the sweet comforts of her small room. The morning sunshine warmed the cozy space, trickling through the window. The smell of bacon and eggs drifted in, Herm's finest. Her senses relaxed into the surreal pleasure. The ankle was still throbbing a painful rhythm, but somehow she didn't mind as much.

She pushed herself up against the crisp pillowcase, reassuring herself that what had happened the previous night was indeed fact, not a dream. Max was dead. Pete was arrested for his murder and the attempted murder of her mother, not to mention Pilar's, Austin's and her father's. Mom was recovering slowly. Her father would be going back to jail, most likely, for concealing his ill-gotten gains, but Jude said he did not think Cyrus would serve much time.

Was there a chance she could build some sort of relationship with her father? Her pride said no, until she remembered that everyone deserved a chance to redeem themselves. Had she done that with Austin? She was not sure. And that was the thing she was most grateful for... Austin was safe, the whole matter finally over with.

Thinking of him made her sink back against the pillows. He was a different person, more peaceful, his soul settled on a truth that would never be stripped away from him. He'd needed God's grace, and he'd received it in abundance. Her joy gave way to a pang of worry. What would happen now? She'd leave Furnace

Falls, of course, and he'd go on with his life and she hers. They could be friends, since the hurt had dissipated, at least on her part. It should have been solace, but still her spirit was restless.

There was a soft rap on the door. Willow stuck her head in. Her eyes danced with excitement. "How are you, Pilar?" She held up a cold pack. "Brought you more ice for your ankle."

"Thank you. I appreciate your kindness, considering."

"Considering you dumped my brother?"

Pilar flushed hot. "Yes, considering that."

"I'm beginning to thaw on that score. Don't tell Austin, but I think you're actually good for him."

That made Pilar's eyes go wide with surprise, but Willow had already pounced on another subject. "You know...this town is hardly bigger than a postage stamp, but the most unbelievable stuff happens here. All that money," she said with a whistle.

"And the people who almost got killed for it."

Pilar grimaced.

"We should write a book someday," Willow said. "Furnace Falls Follies."

"I'm going to stick to writing about wildflowers." Pilar heard a cadence of excited voices. The words were muffled, but the tone was definitely jolly. "What's going on out there? I hear all kinds of comings and goings."

Willow squealed, clasping Pilar's forearms. "Oh, it's so exciting. Laney went into labor just past midnight. We're all scrambling to run things."

"Is everything okay with her and the baby?"

"More than okay. Right around sunrise, she delivered a baby girl. Isn't that grand? Austin took the phone call. Of course, I had to call back because he was so excited he didn't even get the gender or weight or anything. Not one single detail. Can you imagine? He just disconnected and shouted out that Laney'd had the baby and they were both okay. Typical man." She stood.

Pilar beamed. "Fantastic. Beckett must be over the moon."

"I've spoken to him twice since the birth to get all the pertinent details. The baby is seven pounds four ounces, and they are still undecided about a name. He alternates between terrified and elated. All he can say is, 'She's so tiny, perfect, all the proper parts and in the right proportions.' They both enjoyed a laugh over that one.

"The Duke family never ceases to entertain." Willow wiped her eyes. "Are you up for visitors?"

"Sure," Pilar said. "Who?"

"You'll see." She leaned over and kissed Pilar on the cheek, suddenly more serious. "I'm glad you came to Furnace Falls, even though it was all I could do not to mash you when you first arrived. You made mistakes, but I've been remembering lately that so have I. The old mote in your eye and a beam in mine. Anyway, I'll let the gang in."

She walked to the door. Pilar was exceedingly grateful for Willow's forgiveness.

Grace for the humble.

Thank you, God.

Willow exited, leaving the door partially open. Austin peeked in. "Okay to enter?"

Her pulse skittered. She was acutely aware that her hair hadn't been brushed and she was wearing yet another pair of Willow's borrowed sweats. "Yes, of course."

He opened the door fully and Waffles bounded in, dropping a soggy tennis ball on her bed, Lucy right behind him. He stood on his hind legs, front paws on the covers, slavered her with his tongue as she rubbed his ears. "Oh, I missed you too, Waffles."

"Down, boy. Good manners, remember? Figured it was okay to smuggle them in since Beckett is with Laney and Muffin," Austin said. "We're going to have to find out what that baby's real name is pretty soon, unless maybe they're going to stick with Muffin."

Scrabbling in after Waffles and Lucy came Chunk. He whined in happiness to see her and tried to hoist himself up next to her. She laughed and helped him up.

"Good morning, my sweetie boy," she said, hugging him close. "Are you taking good care of Waffles and Lucy?" A pang of pain reminded her that one of their little family had not been found. Lucy pawed the edges of the bedspread until Pilar patted her.

"And one more," Austin said nonchalantly, interrupting her thoughts. With one hand he brought from behind his back an ecstatic Ethel. The tiny dog quivered with excitement at Pilar's cry of surprise, miniature nose twitching in double time.

"Oh, Ethel," Pilar cried, tears gathering. She gathered the dog in close to Chunk while Waffles sat with his retrieved ball, tail thumping the hardwood. "Where did you find her? I'd given up hope."

"Me too. Turns out she made it to a neighbor's place about a half mile from me, but she lost her collar in the process. He took her in and tended to her until he finally got around to turning on his computer and saw the lost dog notice on the website. Then brought her right over." Austin's eyes were a bit damp, as well. "Not very manly, but to be honest I bawled like a toddler."

She smiled, picturing this big man reunited with his minuscule dog. Love truly did have nothing to do with size. "I'm so happy you're home, Ethel."

"They each got a new bone and chicken broth on their kibble to celebrate." Austin gave all four dogs a pat and received four slurps in return. "Now that we got the band back together and the drama is all over, I wanted to give you something too." With the other hand he'd concealed behind his back, he produced a quaint bouquet of the most exquisite wildflowers. Purple lupine, gold poppies, the delicate desert stars, bursts of color that sparkled nowhere as brightly as they did in the desert. All she could do was admire them in delight. "They're absolutely gorgeous," she said after a moment.

"Don't worry. They aren't from the national park or anything. I got them at Levi's. Willow helped me find them. Too bad they won't last very long."

"That's what makes them extra special. A treasure for the moment. They're just beautiful, thank you."

She noticed his hands were shaking.

He exhaled. "You know what, Pilar? I'm a greedy man."

"What?"

"I don't cotton to the notion that treasure is only 'for the moment' stuff. I want to hang on to my treasures."

She raised an eyebrow. "What do you mean?"

He fingered one of the delicate blossoms. "What I said before about the wildflowers...that they were quitters." He cleared his throat. "I was wrong. They're just waiting for the right moment, like you said. God provided the opportunity for them to flourish. It just took a while, didn't it?"

He seemed lost in thought, gazing at the delicate petals until his eyes raised to meet hers.

"Take a closer look," he said, cheeks suddenly pink against his pale complexion. He pointed to the nosegay.

Confused, she peered into the center of the bouquet. Tied to one stalk of lupine was a glittering object that made her heart thud to a stop. With trembling fingers she pulled out the stalk with the sapphire engagement ring attached. Her ring, the one she'd put on in haste without fully understanding what it meant. Commitment was more than love, it was trust and endurance and forbearance and humility and God's grace. All of which she'd walked away from. Now here it was, the glimmering blue stone, shining like hope in the darkness.

Try as she might, not a single word would come out of her mouth.

He went down on one knee, scooting Waffles out of the way. Was this happening? Was she in the middle of a sweet dream from which she'd awaken any moment?

"I thought I would never see this ring again," she finally whispered. "I didn't think I deserved to, or that you would ever... I mean..."

"Pilar," he said, seizing her hands. "I'm

not the man I was, and you're not the woman you were. Agreed?"

She nodded mutely.

"I've learned I'm full to the brim with pride and stubbornness, and I want to control things and tell God to stay on the sidelines while I handle everything. It's dumb, but I still feel the urge to do that almost every moment. I am probably going to need to work on those problems for the rest of my life, but you know what?" He kissed her thumb, and then each knuckle in turn. "I'm now smart enough to know that I can't live it without you."

"But Austin... I... Last time..."

"Last time you made a mistake leaving me and not trusting me, but I gave you reasons. You know what my biggest mistake was?" He took her hand and kissed her wrist. "Not going after you. I should have turned over every rock and stone until I found you, but instead I let you leave because my pride was bigger than my good sense. We got a second chance, now. How many people can say that?"

She heard the words. They turned over in her ears, then worked their way to her brain and then settled soft as a breeze in her heart. She knew he was waiting for her to answer, but she was simply speechless.

"I love you," he said quietly. "I want you to marry me, if you'll have me, and this time nothing is going to get in the way."

She blinked, but he was still there. It was not a tissue-paper dream. There was her soul mate, on his bended knee, and there was the sapphire ring he untied from the flower stalk, held out to her like a sparkling sunrise.

"I love you, Austin," she breathed.

A tear trickled from his eye, and his voice shook when he answered. "It is the greatest privilege of my life to hear you say that." He took a ragged breath. "I love you too, Pilar. We are going to have such a future together. You, me…and four dogs at last count. Can you stand it?"

She began to laugh and the dogs licked her under the chin.

"Yes, Austin. I can stand it."

He pushed the dogs away and captured her mouth with a kiss.

On the appointed day a month later, there were two brides strolling to meet their grooms in the tiny Furnace Falls church. Mara had been enthusiastic to share the spotlight with Pilar, since neither one of them were much for being the center of attention. As a matter of fact, she'd suggested it the moment Levi told her of Austin's proposal. Delaying the ceremony made it easier for new mother Laney and her nervous new dad Beckett to attend. Plus the postponement had also been beneficial for Pilar's mom to regain some strength after her discharge from the hospital.

"Ready to go meet your husband?" Mara said, linking arms with her father and big brother, Seth.

Pilar nodded, almost unable to speak as she took her own mother's hand. Jude was pushing Bernadette's wheelchair since she was still too weak to stand for any length of time. Her smile was brilliant though, and she pulled a cell phone out of her bag and took a picture of Pilar.

"You look so beautiful," she said, gazing at the simple white veil and the elegant tea-length dress. "I want to show your father."

Father. He'd been so far removed from her life for so long, it would be a slow rebuilding process if they were able to fashion any kind of close relationship at all after he'd served his six-month sentence. As Austin had said of their own amazing journey, they'd gotten a second chance from God. Who was she to turn her back on that?

Heart brimming, she tucked her mother's hand into her own and held the simple white rose bouquet, speckled with wildflowers Austin had delivered to her via Willow before the ceremony.

When the doors opened, she did not remember a moment of the pain she'd felt before when she'd bolted from the church. There was only joy now, in the filled pews of expectant faces that turned to greet them: Jude, Aunt Kitty, Beckett side to side with Laney, both beaming over the precious infant bundled in her arms. Willow and Mara's sister, Corinne, in elegant silk dresses with mini bouquets, preceding them down the aisle.

And at the altar, Levi, face wreathed in an unusual smile, waited for Mara. Austin, blond hair neatly combed, handsome in a suit and tie, stood with his brother, all-over eagerness for his bride to join him.

"Are you ready?" Mara said again, her own elation shining in her dark eyes.

Pilar nodded. "Absolutely," she said. Blinking back tears, she went to meet her groom, thanking God for second chances.

* * * * *

If you enjoyed this story, look for these other books by Dana Mentink:

Framed in Death Valley
Missing in the Desert

Dear Reader,

Have you ever gotten a second chance to fix a mistake? Who wouldn't want an opportunity to mend something broken, or have a "do-over" for a relationship gone wrong? That is one of the many blessings God gives sometimes, the precious opportunity to make a U-turn and try again. This story is full of second chances: Pilar and Austin, Mara and Levi, a new baby for Beckett and Laney, the unwanted dog, Chunk, who finds his forever home. Of course, in fiction, it's easy to make those "do-overs" wind up in happily-ever-afters. Maybe that's why I loved writing this book of wrongs turned into "rights" and dead ends into beautiful new roads.

If you follow me on social media, you know that Death Valley is a place near and dear to my heart after our recent travels there. It is a spot where you can see God's handwriting everywhere, in the wildflowers, the rock formations, the tenacious animals that survive in one of the earth's most hostile locations. I look forward to the next three books set in this magnificent location. Thank you for coming along with me!

As always, if you'd like to contact me, you can reach out on social media or via my website at www.danamentink.com. There is a physical address there as well if you'd like to correspond by snail mail.

God bless you!
Dana